The Trouble With Sunbathers

By the Same Author

Novels

The Restraint of Beasts
All Quiet on the Orient Express
Three to See the King
The Scheme For Full Employment
Explorers of the New Century
The Maintenance of Headway
A Cruel Bird Came to the Nest and Looked In
The Field of the Cloth of Gold
The Forensic Records Society
Tales Of Muffled Oars

Stories

Once in a Blue Moon
Only When the Sun Shines Brightly
Screwtop Thompson and Other Tales

The Trouble With Sunbathers

Magnus Mills

QUOQS

Quoqs Publishing for Magnus Mills

First Published 2020

Kindle Direct Publishing

This book is work of a fiction. The names and characters are from the author's imagination and any resemblance to actual persons or zoological species, living or dead, is entirely coincidental.

No part of this publication may be reproduced in any form or means without prior written permission from the publisher.

Cover designed by Richard Moody

Cover illustration by Rawpixel

Copyright © Magnus Mills 2020

10 9 8 7 6 5 4 3 2 1

All rights reserved.

For Phil

1.

There's no doubt that the president was a man of extraordinary ability. He could find a solution to any problem set before him. His decision to purchase the British Isles was widely acclaimed as an act of genius. It solved our financial difficulties at a stroke and in consequence we will always owe a debt of gratitude to the president. Even so, he could never claim to understand the British people. Not properly. He thought he knew what we wanted, but actually he didn't.

2.

Rupert and I had done quite well out of 'the purchase' (as it was known at the time). We were in charge of the western gate and enjoyed all the benefits that went with the job. The four main gates had been inaugurated on the day Great Britain was officially declared a national park. They were elaborate structures of wrought iron and looked rather imposing when they were closed. Their purpose, nonetheless, was largely symbolic. The park was supposed to be open to anyone who wished to visit, and it followed that the gates should likewise remain open at all times. It so happened that the gates were fitted with locks, but there were no keys because keys weren't required. The gates stood open on a permanent basis and it was the role of the gatekeepers to greet people as they passed through. Or at least give them a friendly nod. It was undemanding work, but Rupert and I performed our duties without complaint.

After a while, however, we heard a rumour that the keepers of the southern gate had slightly altered their work practice. They'd taken to closing their gate on odd occasions for no apparent reason. Soon we learnt that the northern and eastern gates were similarly being closed at random intervals, so after a lengthy debate we decided to try it for ourselves. It didn't take long to deduce the reason for the closures. Queues of would-be travellers quickly built up on each side of the gate, and when we finally opened it we were rewarded for our troubles with all kinds of tips and gratuities. In short, we'd discovered that a gate that opened and closed had a higher economic value than one that stayed open all the time. What amazed me was the way people would happily part with their money when they could plainly see we didn't really deserve it.

I wasn't fully at ease with this situation

and eventually I voiced my concern to Rupert.

'I'm not sure if this is what the president had in mind,' I said. 'Don't you think we're rather taking advantage of his generosity?'

'On the contrary,' Rupert replied. 'I think he'd probably approve of what we're doing. After all, he puts a cash value on everything.'

Rupert had a point there. The park may have been free to enter, but once inside people were subject to all sorts of additional charges, from the hire of a paddleboat to a tour of a former industrial region. As the president stated in his frequent pronouncements: 'We always make it pay.'

So it was that I gradually acquiesced to the systematic opening and closing of the gate. This necessarily involved a degree of careful timing, so as not to seem to be deliberately obstructing access to the park, so as not to inconvenience passers-by, and so as not to attract too much attention to the closures. Rupert soon proved adept at making these judgements, so generally I left the precise details to him. All the same, I should make it clear that we never pushed our luck too far when we conducted these operations. Our dealings with the travelling public were exemplary, and if a tip wasn't forthcoming then we would simply let it go. Furthermore, there were long periods when we left the gate open as a matter of course, for instance when we embarked on one of our excursions.

These took place a couple of times a week. What we liked to do was wander into the park for a mile or so and examine the condition of the highway. This stretch had once been known as the Great West Road, but nowadays the tarmac was cracked, the white lines were fading and the signs were rusty. The reason was obvious. When the purchase was first agreed, one of the terms stipulated that no changes would be made to any aspect of the landscape (the only exception being the four new gates, which incidentally were all designed by the president's son-in-law). The intention was that Britain should remain preserved forever in its existing state, but no allowances had been made for such factors as decay, erosion and subsidence. The inevitable result was what now lay before us: slowly but surely the road was vanishing into obscurity.

'Must be like this across the whole country,' observed Rupert as we sauntered along one fine spring afternoon. 'Imagine all those motorways and dual carriageways steadily succumbing to the force of nature.'

'The sooner the better,' I said. 'I like the sound of that.'

Rupert crouched low and glanced across the tarmac.

'Ah yes,' he said with satisfaction. 'I can see the first blades of grass pushing through.'

He stood up again just as a car came trundling along from the east. It was a large, black, left-hand drive sedan, no doubt hurriedly imported in the final few days before the purchase. We'd seen this car several times before. As it drew near the driver slowed down a little and wound open his window.

'Wanna ride?' he called, before adding, 'Oh hi!' as he recognised us from the gate.

He didn't await our reply, but we gave him a cheery wave and he continued in a westerly direction. This cry of 'Wanna ride?' had become commonplace in recent years and was due to the diminishing number of vehicles on the road. The last British car manufacturers had all gone out of business at the time of the fiscal crisis, along with the service companies, the repair shops and the suppliers of spare parts. As various models became obsolete and the national stock dwindled, people whose cars were still running felt obliged to offer rides to those whose weren't. I should add that although they felt obliged to offer them, in most cases they actually didn't. Instead they would call 'Wanna ride?' through their window before driving on. The custom was broadly tolerated as a sort of ironic comment on industrial decline, but occasionally it wore a bit thin, especially when it was raining. We knew, however, that our man in the black sedan meant no offence and would certainly have stopped if we'd flagged him down for help. Moreover, he wasn't speeding, which was very much frowned upon these days.

'Traffic's light today,' said Rupert. 'We might as well leave the gate open for the time being.'

'Alright,' I replied. 'Shall we go a bit further then?'

Rupert agreed and we continued our stroll. We passed the tyre storage depot (no longer required) and the disused brewery, then the land opened up at the beginning of the railway sidings. Neither of us had been this far east for a while, so we were surprised when presently we came upon a large billboard at the side of the road.

'That's odd,' I said. 'I thought billboards weren't allowed.'

'They're not,' said Rupert. 'I'm afraid we'll have to report this.'

'But we can't really, can we?'

'Why not?'

'Well,' I said, 'how would we like it if somebody reported us for closing the gate?'

'That's different,' he countered. 'We don't do any harm to the landscape when we close the gate, whereas this counts as a major change. It's not allowed. It goes against the terms of the purchase.'

I was about to argue that the terms of the purchase had nothing to do with mere gatekeepers when I was suddenly rendered speechless. As we'd approached the billboard we'd been at an angle to it so we couldn't actually read what it said. Now we drew level and its message was spelt out in bold letters:

> WE'LL MAKE THEM WORK!
> WE'LL WORK THEM HARD!
> WE'LL MELT THE BRITISH
> DOWN FOR LARD!

There was no accompanying picture or illustration. We stood peering at the billboard in astonishment.

'So that's what they think of us,' said Rupert at length.

'Seems that way,' I answered.

Just then I became aware of a vehicle coming along from the east. I could hear the tyres rumbling and at any moment I expected to hear a cry of 'Wanna ride?' (which I certainly wasn't in the mood for). Instead, however, the vehicle pulled up at the roadside. It was another black sedan. The driver got out and walked over to join us.

'Hey,' he said.

'Alright,' we both replied.

He nodded at the billboard.

'Impressive, eh?'

Rupert and I glanced at one another.

'Yes,' I murmured, 'I suppose you could call it impressive.'

The newcomer looked at me inquisitively.

'So are you impressed or not?'

'Well,' I said, 'it's sort of.......'

'Not very subtle,' said Rupert.

The man appeared genuinely taken aback.

'I'm disappointed,' he said. 'We thought it was extremely subtle. You see, it's an advertisement for a physical training regime.'

'In Britain?'

'Yes.'

'You mean work them hard until they melt?'

'That's the idea. Kind of.'

'Oh.'

'So don't be concerned,' he added brightly. 'Nobody's planning to exterminate all of you.'

'Didn't say they were.'

Rupert's rather blunt rejoinder temporarily silenced the man. He considered the words for a few seconds, then abruptly changed the subject and introduced himself.

'Carruthers,' he said. 'Just arrived from the east.'

'Rupert,' said Rupert.

'Staying long?' I enquired.

'Depends,' came the reply. 'I have a few matters to sort out in this region and I'm not sure how long it's going to take.'

'Oh, yes?'

'But in any event I guess you'll see quite a lot of me in the next few weeks.'

'How do you mean?'

'Well, you're the guys from the gate, aren't you?'

'Yes.'

'Can't help but see me then, can you?'

He gave us both a nod and a smile before returning to his car. He'd left the engine idling, so the instant he closed the door he was off. We watched him recede into the distance.

'Very self-assured, wasn't he?' I remarked.

'"Brash" would be a better description,' said Rupert.

'I wonder how he knew we were from the gate.'

'He's probably seen us there.'

'But he told us he'd just arrived from the east.'

'Oh, yes, you're right.'

'And he didn't ask us if we wanted a ride.'

'Well, we didn't want one anyway.'

'Suppose not.'

We looked up at the billboard and read the words once more:

WE'LL MAKE THEM WORK!
WE'LL WORK THEM HARD!
WE'LL MELT THE BRITISH
DOWN FOR LARD!

'Somebody's put a lot of thought into that,' I said.

'Or none at all,' said Rupert.

3.

Life at the western gate continued as normal, though over the following few weeks the passing traffic became increasingly sparse. It seemed that more and more people were neglecting the park, preferring to stay on the coast where large numbers had settled permanently. I should explain that in the final days before the purchase a popular misunderstanding had arisen. It was wrongly believed that the coastal areas would somehow be outside the new park's jurisdiction, and this had triggered a mass exodus towards the coast. In desperation, the authorities took measures to stem the flow. Public announcements were made explaining that nothing really had changed, that people were free to come and go as they pleased, and that if they abandoned the interior it would soon become a vast empty wilderness. By this time, however, the migrants had begun to put down roots and were reluctant to move again. In consequence, the entire coastline of Britain was now crowded with people, while the prediction about the empty interior was rapidly coming true. Most of the travellers who passed through our gate nowadays were visitors from other countries: the British themselves didn't appear very interested.

As a matter of fact, some of the above-mentioned visitors had made themselves quite at home. They too were free to come and go as they pleased, and it was a privilege they exercised with increasing frequency. Some could even be counted as regulars. Guys in black sedans were an especially common sight and it was they who provided most of our customers at the gate. The majority drove through, tipped us occasionally, and then continued on their journey.

One morning, however, we spotted a black sedan parked at the roadside about three hundred yards away to the west. The weather was pleasant and we'd noticed a slight increase in the volume of traffic. Rupert had decided, therefore, to put our gate closure system into operation. During the next hour or so, several vehicles passed by. Some tipped, some didn't, just as we'd come to expect. In the meantime, the black sedan remained where it was. We were just beginning to wonder if it had broken down when suddenly it began moving towards the gate. Rupert and I were both inside the gatehouse. We waited for the car to come to a complete halt, then I went out to greet the driver. Which was when I recognised Carruthers sitting behind the wheel. I gave him a friendly nod and opened the gate to let him through. He wound down his window.

'Hey,' he said.

'Hey,' I replied. 'How's the training regime?'

'Well, I can tell you this: it doesn't include sunbathing.'

'Pardon?'

'They're all sunbathing back there on the coast. Great crowds of them on the beaches. Haven't they got anything better to do?'

'Probably not actually.'

Carruthers shook his head. 'We'll have to see about that. Incidentally, how much do you charge for opening the gate?'

'Oh, there's no charge,' I said quickly. 'It's free.' (This was our stock answer, devised by Rupert.)

'Is that so?' he said.

'No charge,' I repeated.

'In that case you might as well leave it open.'

With those words Carruthers smiled and drove away. All the while, Rupert had been observing proceedings from the gatehouse window. Now he came and joined me outside, and I told him what Carruthers had said.

'He certainly seems to have all the answers,' Rupert remarked. 'By the way, did you notice the field binoculars lying on his passenger seat?'

'No,' I replied. 'I didn't.'

'Superpowered, by the look of them.'

'Really?'

'Must have been spying on us.'

'Surely not.'

'That was why he was parked up the road,' said Rupert. 'Watching us opening and closing the gate.'

Rupert's allegation struck me as rather far-fetched, but actually I couldn't think of any other reason why someone would carry a pair of binoculars with them. There was no interesting wildlife in the park: just the usual fauna and flora of the British Isles. Just then, though, I happened to glance to the east and saw the same black sedan parked at the side of the road about a quarter of a mile beyond the gate. It was facing away from us. I pointed it out to Rupert.

'Who's he spying on now then?' I

enquired.

'Don't know,' he said.

We continued peering at the vehicle, and a minute later a tiny figure appeared from somewhere to the right and crossed the road.

'Is that him?'

'Can't tell at this distance,' said Rupert. 'Shame we haven't any binoculars ourselves.'

Next moment the car moved away, heading east.

After a brief discussion we decided that Carruthers probably hadn't been spying on us after all. Even so, we agreed it would be a good idea to leave the gate open for the time being.

4.

We sometimes tended to forget that ours wasn't the only gate in the west. True, it was the most well known. Designed by the president's son-in-law, it was one of four ceremonial gates that marked the inauguration of the national park. Actually, however, there were countless other exits and entrances as well as ours. This was a fact that Rupert and I accepted only reluctantly. We liked to think that our gate was the most important in the region, and we hardly gave a thought to the 'minor' gates (as we called them).

We were somewhat surprised, therefore, to learn that an incident had recently occurred at one of the other gates. From what we could gather, a couple of men had pulled up in a black sedan, parked in a lay-by at the side of the road, then closed the gate. They spent the next couple of hours questioning drivers as they arrived, prior to letting them through. The gate was on a quiet road about five miles away from ours and was never known to have been closed before. Needless to say, the two guys weren't official gatekeepers (the minor gates were all unmanned). Nevertheless, passing drivers obediently answered their questions. Apparently they were enquiring whether anybody had noticed anything unusual during their travels. What constituted 'unusual' wasn't explained, but the answer was invariably 'no' and drivers were then allowed to continue on their journeys. Eventually the two men had suspended their operation and driven away.

Rupert and I only heard about the episode second-hand because one of our regulars happened to mention it in passing. He usually came through our gate on a Wednesday. The rest of the week he travelled mostly along the coast road, but on the previous Friday he'd decided to take an alternative route, just for a change, and he'd ended up at the gate where the two men were making their enquiries. It seemed they'd detained him for about ten minutes, which was no major inconvenience, but next time he saw me and Rupert he assumed we were going to question him as well. The first we knew about it was when he pulled up beside our gatehouse. I stepped out to greet him, wondering why he'd bothered to stop when the gate was wide open. As I said before, he was one of our regulars. He was quite friendly as well as being a generous tipper, and he always liked to exchange some banter with me and Rupert. He wound down his window.

'I've been thinking about this,' he said, 'and it's all the wrong way round.'

'Oh yes?' I replied.

'It would be better if you itemised the things I might have noticed, then ask me whether I've noticed any of them.'

'Suppose so.'

'Or perhaps give me a list of items to tick off.'

'Okay.'

'It's too vague simply to ask whether I've noticed anything unusual.'

'Yes.'

I had to admit that today's banter left me completely baffled. I gazed blankly at the man in the car, and he gazed at me.

'Alright,' he said at length. 'Go ahead. Ask away.'

'Ask what?'

'Ask if I've noticed anything unusual.'

'Well, have you?'

'No.'

All the while, Rupert had been viewing proceedings through the gatehouse window. Now he came out and joined us.

'Nice day,' he said. 'What's it like on the coast?'

'Same as here,' said the man, 'except they're all sunbathing.'

'Yes, we heard that.'

'Plainly got nothing better to do.'

'No.'

He peered at the pair of us.

'You know what,' he said. 'I've never been certain which of you two is in charge.'

'Me,' said Rupert.

'Oh, well, perhaps you could mention to those other fellows my suggestion for a list of what I might have noticed. It would be so much easier for all concerned. Far less time-consuming.'

Rupert and I looked at one another, then back at the man in the car.

'Sorry,' I said. 'What other fellows?'

'Those two at the other gate. You know, near the MovieDrome. They had a black sedan parked in a lay-by. They wanted to know if I'd noticed anything unusual and they wouldn't open the gate until I said 'no'. They kept me there for ten minutes and I'm sure I wasn't the only one they held up.'

Just then another car appeared from the

west, so I stepped out to wave it through the gate. To my surprise, however, it pulled up behind the first car, whose driver glanced in his mirror.

'I'd better get going,' he said. 'Pass that on, will you?'

We gave him a nod and a smile and he went on his way. The second car pulled forward and the driver wound down his window. On the spur of the moment I decided to try an experiment.

'Morning, sir,' I said. 'Would you mind telling me if you happen to have noticed anything unusual in your travels?'

5.

Over the next couple of weeks we left the gate open at all times. This didn't prevent cars from stopping beside the gatehouse and the drivers expectantly winding down their windows. Out of sheer curiosity, Rupert and I played along with this new practice and enquired whether they'd noticed anything unusual. The answer was unfailingly 'no', and then they'd continue on their journey. At one point we considered presenting them with a list of what they might have noticed, but we soon realized we couldn't because we didn't know what we were supposed to be looking out for. We'd received no official word on the matter and as far as we were concerned it was all simply a game to help pass the time. Nonetheless, it quickly became apparent that passing drivers took the matter quite seriously. Being asked if they'd noticed anything unusual evidently made them feel important, and by the end of the second week the majority of drivers were pulling up at our gate as a matter of routine.

We swiftly learned that the two men at the other gate hadn't ceased their activities. Far from it: they were there almost every day and people were becoming quite accustomed to their enquiries. Furthermore, the fact that there was generally less traffic on the roads these days seemed to make the remaining travellers feel as though they belonged to some exclusive fraternity, and that they were all united in the quest to spot something unusual. For the moment, the answer was an emphatic 'no', but we soon began to wonder how long this would last.

'What are we going to do,' pondered Rupert, 'if something unusual is reported?'

'Not sure,' I said. 'I suppose we could make a note of it in the log.'

Meanwhile, we continued our strolls into the park. We didn't always stick to the Great West

Road: sometimes we ventured along one of the minor roads that joined it on either side. These led us through neglected trading estates and residential areas, past goods yards, playing fields and public gardens, all of which were gradually blending into a vast hinterland of thorny scrub, grass and trees. We paused to gaze sadly at deserted pubs, the names of forgotten landlords displayed above their doorways, and their signs swinging listlessly in the breeze: The Live And Let Live, The Ring of Bells, The Wheatsheaf, The Royal Oak, The Swan, The Cross Hands, The Globe, The Rising Sun and The Masons Arms.

'Nobody even bothered to board up the windows,' observed Rupert. 'They must have known they were never coming back.'

'Shame really,' I said. 'I used to like these places.'

'Well, I'm afraid they've all gone.'

'There are still plenty of pubs on the coast.'

'Yes, but they're not the same.'

'No.'

'Actually, they're all the same. They're different to these, but they're all the same.'

'As each other?'

'Yes,' said Rupert. 'They've got one common purpose: they're for sunbathers to quench their thirst.'

'Not for the likes of us then?'

'No.'

The closures were a great shame, but we knew there was nothing we could do about them. Still, it didn't stop us from gazing with fondness at formerly thriving establishments. Which was how, one afternoon, we found ourselves standing outside The Cross Hands. Once a favourite haunt of ours, we'd especially liked it because it stood opposite the municipal fire station, so there was always some exciting spectacle to watch through the window. Every night, accompanied by gruff shouts and the urgent ringing of a bell, fire engines would come charging out of the gates with their lights flashing and sirens blaring. They'd rush off down the road and disappear headlong into the darkness, only to return a little while later, quietly and calmly, as if all their energy had been expended. The proximity of the fire station meant there was never any trouble in The Cross Hands. Most of the firemen drank there when they were off-duty, so naturally they wanted it to remain intact. At the least hint of a disturbance, several burly officers would appear in the doorway and enquire if everything was alright. This was usually enough to quell any unruliness. Of course, in recent years the fire station had been decommissioned, but the building itself looked as magnificent as ever. It was a traditional red brick structure with a high watchtower overlooking the entire neighbourhood.

'Must be able to see a long way from up there,' said Rupert. 'Shall we go and have a look?'

'I should imagine it's all locked up,' I said.

'You know: health and safety.'

'Doubt it,' he replied. 'Nobody cares about that sort of thing any more.'

'No, I suppose not.'

'And, in any case, it's hardly dangerous.'

'No.'

'Shall we give it a try then?'

'Okay.'

We crossed the road and entered the main yard of the fire station. The building was empty: all the fire engines had gone. We could now see the foot of the watchtower, where there was a steel door. It appeared to be slightly ajar, so we headed towards it. As we drew near, however, we suddenly heard footsteps descending a metal staircase. Next moment, the door opened and Carruthers emerged. He was carrying a pair of binoculars.

'Ah,' he said, when he saw us. 'The guys from the western gate.'

Judging by the look on his face, he wasn't

expecting to bump into anybody, but there again neither were we.

'We noticed the door was open,' said Rupert. 'We'd thought we'd better check it.'

'We didn't see your car,' I added.

'I haven't got it with me,' said Carruthers. 'I came across country.'

'You mean on foot?'

'Yes.'

'Good going,' I said. 'All part of the training regime?'

He paused for a few seconds to consider the question. More than a few seconds actually, and I got the impression he was trying to think back to our previous encounter. Or perhaps the one before.

'That's the idea,' he said at length. 'Kind of.'

Carruthers placed his binoculars on a nearby bench. Next he produced a bunch of keys from his pocket, selected one, then closed and locked the steel door. He put the keys back in his pocket and picked up the binoculars.

I raised my eyes towards the top of the watchtower.

'Must be a good view.'

'Yes,' he said. 'You can see for miles.'

He smiled and nodded and moved away as if to go, but then a thought struck me.

'While you were up there,' I said, 'did you spot anything unusual?'

Carruthers stopped in mid-stride and turned around.

'You mean did I notice anything unusual?' he asked.

'Well, yes,' I replied. 'It's all the same, isn't it?'

'No, it's not the same,' he said. 'There's a subtle difference between spotting something you're looking for and noticing something you're not looking for.'

'Oh,' I said. 'Is there?'

'Certainly.'

'I've never given it much thought.'

'Odd, really,' he continued. 'We share the same language and yet there are so many subtle differences.'

'Yes, I suppose so.'

He patted his pocket where the keys were, as if to make sure they were still there.

'By the way,' he enquired, 'did you come here on foot as well?'

'Yes,' I said. 'We're supposed to have a vehicle that goes with the job, but it's in dock at present. There's a vital part missing. It's unobtainable.'

Carruthers shook his head.

'Same old story,' he said. "Britain stands alone'.'

'How do you mean?'

'The shortage of spare parts,' he announced, 'is a prime example of British obstinacy. Or British exceptionalism, if you like:

call it what you will. The shortage was predicted years ago. We all saw it coming and the obvious solution was staring us in the face. Universal spare parts! Absolute simplicity and uniformity! Problem solved at a stroke! It made sense. Every country adopted universal spare parts because they could be interchanged and used in any vehicle. Every country, that is, except Great Britain. Great Britain refused to cooperate. Great Britain insisted that only British parts could be fitted in British vehicles. So what happened when the parts ran out? Everything ground to a halt.'

Carruthers ceased speaking and gazed at Rupert and me with undisguised self-satisfaction. It didn't seem to occur to him that we hadn't requested a lecture on the decline of British motor manufacturing. Or that perhaps we didn't really care one way or another. Neither was it clear whether he expected us to thank him for the information he'd provided. Nevertheless, there was one fact I felt I ought to point out.

'It's still unobtainable,' I said, 'whatever the reason.'

Carruthers smiled again.

'Well,' he said, 'walking never harmed anybody.'

With those words he headed across the yard and out into the road, where he turned left. After that, we quickly lost sight of him.

'Do you realise,' said Rupert, 'he never answered your question?'

'What question?'

'About whether he'd spotted anything unusual?'

'You mean noticed.'

'Oh, yes, noticed.'

'No, you're quite right,' I said. 'He didn't.'

6.

We decided to go back by a slightly different route, one we hadn't tried before, so we left the fire station and took a path that cut behind The Cross Hands and over a railway footbridge. Here we turned right. We walked between two rows of houses, crossed another road and then found ourselves on open scrubland. This looked as if it had once been some kind of recreation ground, but it was now markedly overgrown. There were small trees dotted here and there among burgeoning thorn bushes, and the grass was long and wavy. At one point we passed a large concrete rectangle, possibly the site of a former clubhouse, and even this had saplings pushing through it. We could just make out the remains of a narrow approach road, so we followed it to a junction at the far end.

'Do you know where we are?' I said.

'Pretty much,' said Rupert. 'We just cross over here and keep bearing right and we'll come out on the Great West.'

We entered yet more thorny scrub, but now it was even thicker than before. A dilapidated sign told us this was a piece of land that had been awaiting development for several years. According to various notices pasted on top of each other, somebody wanted to build a hypermarket, but they couldn't get planning permission, so they applied again and once more they were refused.

'A prime example of British obstinacy,' declared Rupert.

'Or British exceptionalism,' I said. 'Call it what you will.'

We both had a good laugh about that.

Despite the land being undeveloped, we soon discovered that there was a path across it. Not a proper waymarked path: somebody had merely cleared a trail through the undergrowth by trampling it underfoot.

'Must have been here quite recently,' said Rupert. 'These twigs and branches are still green.'

'And more than one person,' I added. 'Looks as if they were on a route march.'

'Maybe it was part of the training regime that Carruthers told us about.'

'Yes, maybe.'

'Well, they're certainly a tough bunch, if this is any indication.'

We'd just come upon a large clump of thorn bushes which appeared to have been simply brushed aside by some unstoppable force. There was more flattened undergrowth ahead of us, as well as numerous broken saplings. All this destruction cleared the way for Rupert and me. The going was easy and in consequence we soon arrived at the Great West Road, just as he'd predicted. Over at the far side we could see a wooden fence that had been smashed down, and beyond it more trampled ground.

'Sheer vandalism,' said Rupert. 'There's no need for that.'

7.

By the time we got back to the gatehouse it was almost dark and we were ready for supper. As usual, Rupert set about preparing a meal. Meanwhile, I kept out of the way. Rupert and I had a long-standing arrangement whereby he did all the cooking and I did all the washing-up. It generally worked well, the only problem being that Rupert often accused me of 'hovering' around the kitchen as mealtimes approached. I wasn't aware that I was particularly 'hovering', but evidently my presence was too much for Rupert, so I'd learned to keep clear of him until everything was ready. My only option was to wander around in the immediate vicinity of the gatehouse and await his call. Which was how I came to be standing by the western gate, gazing at the night sky.

Darkness had now fallen, but it was still a

little early for stars. Just above the horizon in the south, however, I could see a kind of flickering. This revived a faint memory of something once familiar that had long since faded into oblivion, though for the moment I couldn't quite put my finger on it. The flickering continued for several minutes, then ceased for a short time, then resumed again, at which point Rupert called me in.

'Been doing anything useful?' he asked. (He made the same enquiry every evening.)

'Yes,' I said. 'I've been oiling the hinges on the gate.'

'Good.'

We sat down at the table where our supper was waiting. We ate in silence, and I took the opportunity to ponder the flickering in the sky. Then all at once I remembered what it was.

'You know the MovieDrome,' I said. 'Has it reopened?'

'Shouldn't think so,' said Rupert. 'It's full

of abandoned cars, isn't it?'

'Oh yes. I'd forgotten about them.'

'Why do you ask?'

'Well, I thought I saw that flickering we used to see when they were showing a film.'

'What, just now?'

'Yes.'

'But they can't have reopened it. People stopped going there when they couldn't find a parking space.'

'Unless they've fixed all those broken down cars.'

Rupert shook his head.

'Very doubtful,' he said. 'Most of them were beyond repair. That's why they were abandoned in the first place.'

'The shortage of spare parts?'

'Correct.'

After supper we went outside and peered at the southern horizon. To my mild annoyance, the flickering had now stopped.

'Maybe it's the intermission,' I suggested.

We waited a short while, standing in the gloom and squinting southward, then sure enough the flickering resumed again. It was actually quite mesmerising to observe, and we remained standing there transfixed for about ten minutes until abruptly the flickering ceased again. This time it failed to resume.

'Must have been quite a short film,' said Rupert. 'Probably that newsreel they used to keep showing about Lee Montana.'

'Oh, yes!' I exclaimed. 'Lee Montana! She'd slipped completely out of my mind!'

'Well, I don't know how,' said Rupert. 'A couple of years ago she was all you ever talked about.'

'And you.'

'Alright,' he admitted. 'And me.'

Lee Montana was the unknown nineteen year old actress who'd auditioned along with hundreds of other hopefuls for the title role in an adventure film called 'Girl On An Elephant'. She duly landed the part and after a lengthy photo shoot received an advance pay cheque for one million dollars. She was then sent to Africa to learn how to ride an elephant, but by the time the film crew arrived she'd vanished, never to be heard from again. Her disappearance sparked a flurry of speculation in the press. Some derided it as a blatant publicity stunt. Others claimed she'd been abducted, or even enslaved. Whatever the reason, filming was abandoned and the crew were all sent home. A little later, however, it transpired that a rival film company had managed to obtain about ten minutes of grainy footage of a girl riding an elephant through the savannah, accompanied by some ostriches, some zebra and young giraffe. Nobody was sure if the girl on the elephant really was Lee Montana. The fact that she was riding bareback after only a few weeks' instruction made some people highly dubious. Nonetheless, the ten minute newsreel was shown repeatedly in cinemas over the next year or so, usually between the adverts and the main feature, and Lee Montana swiftly became a household name.

These events had occurred before the purchase. Now, of course, everything was different. All the newspapers had folded and the cinemas were closed. The days when there were film stars with names like Lee Montana had apparently gone forever.

I gave a sigh.

'I wonder what happened to her?'

'Can't imagine,' said Rupert.

'Doesn't bear thinking about.'

'No.'

'Do you suppose they're really still showing that newsreel?'

'I don't know,' he said, 'but I'll tell you what we'll do. Next time we go for a stroll, why don't we head over to the MovieDrome and have a look?'

'Alright.'

'And on the way we can call at the other gate and see what those guys in the black sedan are up to.'

8.

As it turned out, this plan had to be put on hold. Early the following morning we heard a vehicle pull up by the gatehouse. I glanced casually through the window and saw a van with the words PARK AUTHORITY emblazoned along its side panels.

'Good grief,' I said. 'Martin's come to see us.'

Martin was supposed to be our supervisor, but we'd only actually met him once before. He'd paid us a visit on the day we'd taken over as gatekeepers, promising he'd be in regular touch, but we hadn't seen hide nor hair of him since then. He never even sent us instructions, and we'd gradually realized we were on our own. His apparent shirking of responsibility didn't really bother us as it gave us a free hand to operate the gate as we wished. To tell the truth we'd got quite accustomed to not seeing him. We always assumed that there was nothing to worry about, that everything was under control, and that the absent Martin found the arrangement quite satisfactory. Today, though, he emerged from his van wearing the hunted look of someone who'd just had his holiday interrupted. Rupert and I stepped out to meet him.

'Morning lads,' he said with an apologetic smile. 'Everything okay?'

'Yes, thanks,' we replied in unison.

'The gate's looking very spick-and-span.'

'It needs painting,' said Rupert.

'Ah. Does it? Oh. Yes. Well, I dare say we can get some paint sent over in short order.'

We gazed at Martin, both wondering why he'd come to see us.

'And some painters,' he added, 'if you like.'

'Thanks,' said Rupert. 'Did you get our memorandum?'

'Yes, it's being attended to.'

'It's just that we never received a reply.'

'Oh really? Remind me what it was about again, can you?'

'The spare part for our vehicle.'

Martin gave us another apologetic smile.

'Don't talk to me about spare parts,' he said. 'They're my worst nightmare. We send out requests and they come back unanswered.'

'So the part's unobtainable?'

'I'm afraid so. Just for the time being. Sorry.'

While we'd been standing there I'd noticed that Martin was sporting a very healthy tan.

'Been sunbathing?' I enquired.

'Yes,' he said. 'Well, no, not very much actually. Only now and again. Can't really help it back there on the coast, not with all that sunshine, and of course there are people who don't know when enough is enough. Sunbathing dawn till dusk, some of them, week in, week out. Doesn't matter how hot it gets. They'd much rather melt than move into the shade.'

'Oh yes, we've heard about those people,' said Rupert. 'Isn't someone planning to melt them down for lard?'

Martin appeared to give the comment some serious consideration.

'Well, not quite yet,' he said at length.

Just then we heard a car approaching from the east. Martin's van was partially blocking the gateway. He jumped in to move it, but once he'd started the engine he couldn't get it into gear. The oncoming car had started to slow down and looked as though it was going to stop, possibly so that the driver could tell us whether he'd noticed anything unusual in his travels. However, the sight of the van with PARK AUTHORITY emblazoned along the side seemed to bring about a change of mind. The car merely squeezed through the gap and continued on its way. A few seconds later there was a crunch of gears and Martin lurched forward several yards, only to abruptly stop again.

'Clutch is on the way out,' he announced through the window. 'I've ordered a replacement but there's no sign of it as yet.'

After a couple more attempts he finally managed to manoeuvre his van around to the back of the gatehouse.

'Should be alright there for a day or two,' he said, as he rejoined us.

A moment passed while Rupert and I absorbed the full meaning of this remark. Martin was now holding a cake box in one hand and an overnight bag in the other.

'So you're staying with us, are you?' said Rupert.

'Just for a day or two,' came the reply.

As Rupert conducted Martin to the guest room, I tried to fathom the reason for his presence. It occurred to me that somebody might have complained about us accepting tips and gratuities for opening the gate when it was meant to be open anyway. Such a grievance would have been perfectly valid, but it should hardly take two days to deal with. Therefore I immediately ruled it out. We'd already mentioned the spare part for our vehicle, and the fact that the gate needed painting, neither of which could possibly justify a surprise visit, and as far as I knew there were no other outstanding matters.

When the pair of them returned, Martin insisted that we all shared the cake he'd brought with him. He put the box on the table, opened it, and cut three slices. Afterwards he went outside to give the gate a closer inspection.

Once we were alone, Rupert asked me if I'd drawn any conclusions.

'I don't think he's investigating us personally,' I said. 'I'm pretty sure we're in the clear.'

'Well, he's definitely on a mission of some kind,' said Rupert.

'Yes, but what?'

'Beats me.'

There was still more than half of Martin's cake remaining. Rupert cut us another slice each and put the rest of it back in the box. He studied the label on the lid, which said it was the product of more than one country. He put the box in the pantry, then changed his mind and put it back on the table. Rupert seemed to be lost in thought, but then all of a sudden he snapped his fingers triumphantly.

'I've just realized what it is!' he declared. 'The president's coming to see the gate for himself!'

'What?' I said with astonishment. 'You mean a state visit?'

'Correct,' said Rupert.

'Blimey.'

'And it's long overdue when you think about it.'

Rupert certainly had a point there.

It was widely known that the president had

only visited the British Isles on one occasion, and that comprised just a single night's stopover at an airfield many years before. Even so, he always claimed to have developed a deep attachment to the 'old country', as he called it. The president wanted Britain to always remain the same as it was when he'd glimpsed it briefly through the window of his aeroplane. This was why the terms of the purchase stipulated that nothing should be changed, the only exception being the four ceremonial gates (designed by the president's son-in-law) that marked the inauguration of the national park. Evidently, he'd decided it was about time he came to see them with his own eyes.

'Our gate must be the first on the itinerary,' said Rupert. 'No wonder Martin agreed to having it painted.'

Oddly enough, though, Martin didn't say a word about the state visit during his entire sojourn with us. Rupert and I were still eating our cake when he came back into the gatehouse on that first morning. He nodded approvingly and told us to have as much as we liked. Thereafter he spent the day assisting us with our duties, which consisted mainly of greeting motorists as they passed by and offering directions if requested. He showed some interest when people stopped to tell us they hadn't noticed anything unusual in their travels, but he never questioned why they'd bothered stopping in the first place. This led us to believe he knew nothing about the enquiries that were being carried out at the other gate. As far as we could tell, Martin was simply observing our daily routine in order to assure himself that the presidential visit would run smoothly. When eventually darkness fell, the already low rate of traffic dwindled into virtually nothing, and Martin informed us that he was having an early night.

'See you tomorrow,' he said, heading towards the guest room.

After he'd left us, Rupert and I discussed the situation.

'Funny, isn't it?' I said. 'Martin's not being unreasonable or interfering or anything. He's not even as talkative as he was when he first arrived, but I'm still finding it all quite stressful.'

'Same here,' said Rupert, 'but we've only got another day of it and he'll be gone.'

'Let's hope his clutch holds out.'

'Yes.'

9.

When we rose the following morning we found the door of the guest room wide open. The room itself was neat and tidy, but there was no sign of Martin. A short search revealed that he had wandered about a hundred yards along the road into the park. He was peering intently at an ornamental hedge that fronted the Turnpike Senior School for Girls (now closed). We walked up to join him.

The ornamental hedge was once the pride of this section of the road. Motorists used to slow down just to catch sight of it. Some even stopped to take a photograph. In earlier times, the school governors had ensured it was kept clipped and immaculate the whole year round, their diligence reflecting the way the school was run in general. After all, they had a reputation to preserve and appearances counted for everything. Now, though, the governors' efforts were virtually forgotten. The pupils were gone (their parents had moved them to the coast) and the hedge was wild and overgrown. In recent months, Rupert and I had made vague plans to restore it to its former glory, but unfortunately we didn't have any shears. In consequence, it was rapidly going the same way as the rest of the park.

We couldn't quite see why Martin was paying so much attention to the hedge, unless, of course, he too was planning to restore it to its former glory. As we drew near the thought crossed my mind that maybe he intended to spruce it up for the presidential visit. The idea was dashed, however, when I saw exactly what Martin was looking at. Part of the hedge had been completely obliterated. There were scores of broken twigs and branches lying in the road and all across the school's front lawn, where the grass looked as if it had been flattened by many feet. In the middle of the lawn was a statue of Baroness Turnpike, the school's founder. It was leaning at a precarious angle, having apparently been given a hefty shove.

We wished Martin a good morning and then the three of us stood surveying the damage.

'It must be that physical training squad again,' said Rupert. 'Somebody really should have a word with them.'

'This has happened before then, has it?' said Martin.

'Not here,' I said. 'Further up the road.'

'They knocked a fence down,' added Rupert. 'Rather a tough bunch by the look of it.'

Martin shook his head.

'Sheer vandalism,' he remarked. 'There's no need for that.'

'No,' I acknowledged, 'but at least they're not just lolling around sunbathing all day long.'

The moment I spoke I regretted it. I should have known that Martin would be stung by my words. The previous day he'd gone to great lengths to protest that he wasn't guilty of excessive sunbathing. Clearly it had been playing on his mind, yet now I'd probably gone and made him feel worse. To his credit he pretended simply to have misunderstood my glib comparison.

'Well, presumably,' he said, 'you can take part in physical training and get a suntan at the same time.'

'Quite right,' said Rupert, riding swiftly to the rescue. 'One doesn't have to exclude the other.'

'Even so,' Martin continued, 'there's no excuse for wilful destruction. I'll have to make a report to the park authority.'

Interestingly enough, I'd often wondered what the park authority actually did, and indeed who it consisted of. Our only contact with this venerable institution was Martin, whose duties were vague to say the least, and it was hard to imagine the precise roles of those above him in the hierarchy. As far as we knew, the park authority was overseeing the gradual deterioration of what used to be known as Great Britain, and being paid to do so by the president of a distant land. The ramifications were immeasurable. Buildings were crumbling, bridges were collapsing and entire industries were lying in ruins, yet for some reason a localised act of vandalism was deemed worthy of a report. We watched as Martin took a notebook from his pocket and wrote down one or two details.

'By the way,' he said, 'is there a logbook in the gatehouse?'

We affirmed that there was, and he then suggested we made a separate record of the incident.

'Just to cover yourselves,' he explained. 'To prove you've been keeping a lookout.'

'We didn't know we were supposed to keep a lookout,' said Rupert.

'Treat it as an unwritten rule,' said Martin. 'As I said, it's just to cover yourselves.'

Rupert and I didn't pursue the matter

further, and soon the three of us were on our way back to the gatehouse to begin our working day. Once again Martin offered his assistance, so it was he who went out and greeted the first car to roll in from the east. Not surprisingly, the driver had stopped to report the damaged hedge. Martin thanked him for the information and the car was quickly on its way again. Another car followed, and another after that, and each driver stopped for the same reason. As usual, there weren't very many cars on the road. In spite of this, the repeated reports soon became rather tiresome and I could see that Martin was struggling under the pressure.

'It's hard to keep a smile on your face,' he remarked, 'when they all keep telling you the same thing.'

'That's what it's like dealing with the public,' I said, 'but you get used to it after a while.'

Once the eleventh or twelfth car had

stopped Martin suddenly announced that he'd thought of a solution.

'We need to make a sign,' he said. 'I've got all sorts of bits and pieces in the van. I'll go and have a look.'

He disappeared round the back of the gatehouse, returning a quarter of an hour later to show us the results of his handiwork. He was now carrying a red and white sign that said: INCIDENT BEING ATTENDED TO. He looked quite pleased with himself.

'We'll put this in the gap in the hedge,' he said, 'and people won't need to report it anymore.'

'"Incident being attended to",' said Rupert, quoting from the sign. 'Says it all really.'

'Yes,' said Martin. 'It's our stock answer to all complaints and enquiries.'

I accompanied him along to the hedge and we set the sign in position. As we did so I glanced across at Baroness Turnpike (or rather her statue) and thought how forlorn she looked perched there at an acute angle. The lawn that surrounded her was unkempt and hummocky from neglect, there were saplings protruding through the school windows, tiles were falling off the roof, the hedge was overgrown, and it struck me that something ought to be done about it all. Martin, however, was only concerned with his sign.

'That should do the trick,' he said.

Unfortunately he was proved wrong. As the morning passed, more and more people stopped to ask about the incident that was being attended to. They wanted to know what had happened and were somewhat put out when we were unable to provide an answer. In the meantime, of course, we still had to deal with a hardcore of motorists who continued to tell us they hadn't noticed anything unusual during their travels.

Eventually it all became too much for Martin.

'Right,' he said, around about midday.

'Everything seems to be running smoothly here, so I think I'll be on my way.'

He went into the gatehouse to collect his overnight bag, which he then took round to put in his van. A minute later he came trudging back.

'Clutch has gone,' he said. 'Won't move an inch.'

Rupert and I volunteered in turn to try and get the van going, each assuming that we had a better driving technique than Martin (and each other) but both of us actually ended in failure.

'It's no good,' said Martin at length. 'I'll have to leave it here until we get a new clutch.'

'Are you going to stay over then?' I asked.

'No, no,' he replied. 'I'll try and hitch a lift.'

He spoke these words as though it was something he did everyday, and I have to admit I was quite impressed. Patiently he waited beside the gatehouse as cars came and went, speaking to passing drivers in a nonchalant way as various pieces of non-information were exchanged. This went on for about half an hour, then suddenly he came dashing into the gatehouse to grab his bag. He nodded towards a car outside the window.

'That's heading in the right direction,' he informed us. 'I'll be in touch. Enjoy the rest of the cake.'

And then he was gone.

10.

I couldn't stop thinking about Baroness Turnpike, and eventually I expressed my concern to Rupert.

'She looks so undignified leaning over like that,' I said. 'It's a shame when you consider she was such an upright person.'

'I fully agree,' said Rupert, 'but there's nothing we can do about it.'

'Couldn't we have a go at straightening her up a bit?'

'How?'

'Well, we could dig around the base and see if she'll move.'

'But we haven't got any tools.'

'There might be some in Martin's van.'

Rupert peered at me.

'You've got it all thought out, haven't you?' he said.

'I just think we ought to try,' I said. 'It's the least we can do, especially when the president's coming to visit.'

'Oh, yes,' said Rupert. 'I'd forgotten all about him.'

Obviously, if Martin had left his van locked then my plan would have been thwarted. It turned out that he hadn't. We went round and tried the back doors and they opened to reveal a large hoard of equipment, including a couple of spades, a pickaxe, a shovel and a crowbar. There was also a pair of shears and some hedge clippers.

'Ah, good,' I said, 'we can tidy up the hedge as well.'

Rupert was unenthusiastic.

'You're joking,' he said. 'I don't mind having a look at the statue but I'm not touching the hedge. That needs an expert to put it right.'

I decided not to push the idea any further. Later in the afternoon, when the traffic had eased to a trickle, we selected the tools we needed and lugged them along to the school. After slipping through the gap in the hedge, we crossed the lawn and approached the statue. Seen from close-up, Baroness Turnpike looked markedly stern.

'She's not going to thank us for this,' said Rupert.

We began digging around the base of the statue, a task which proved more difficult than I expected. Neither of us had done any proper work for ages and it soon began to tell, particularly as the ground was hard from lack of rain. Nevertheless, we finally made some progress, so we paused for a well-deserved rest.

'If we can loosen the earth just a little bit more,' I said, 'we should be able to get the crowbar underneath.'

'I'm not so sure,' said Rupert. 'There's nothing to lever against.'

Suddenly we were startled by a voice behind us.

'Need any help there?'

We turned and recognised the man who always enjoyed a bit of banter at the gateway. Apparently he'd been driving by and spotted us through the gap in the hedge. We'd been so engaged in our work we hadn't heard him parking his car at the roadside. Now he walked over and joined us.

'By the way,' he said, 'the name's Ambrose.'

Rupert and I introduced ourselves formally, and then we explained what we were trying to do.

'Got a rope?' he asked.

We told him we hadn't.

'I've got one in the car,' he said. 'I always carry it with me in case somebody needs a tow.'

Ambrose plainly intended to take charge of the operation, so we waited while he went to fetch his rope. When he came back he bustled around the statue, checking angles and so forth, before digging out a few more spadefuls of earth. Lastly he tied the rope in position.

'Right,' he said. 'If we all give a good heave we should be able to get somewhere.'

As luck had it, the statue moved at the first attempt. A few additional tugs were required to get it exactly upright, but ultimately we succeeded. Ambrose was clearly a perfectionist, so not until some further adjustments had been made was he completely satisfied. After that it was a simple matter of shovelling all the earth back around the base and packing it down. When we'd finished he coiled his rope into a neat loop and slung it over Baroness Turnpike's left arm, then we all stood back to gaze at our achievement.

'How did she get pushed over in the first place?' Ambrose enquired.

'We think it was that training squad who've been barging around lately,' said Rupert.

'Bunch of vandals,' I added.

'Really?' said Ambrose. 'I haven't seen anybody training.'

'Nor have we, actually,' said Rupert, 'but there's a big billboard down the road advertising the regime.'

'Oh yes, I've read that a few times now you come to mention it: 'We'll make them work and we'll work them hard!"

Ambrose didn't mention the second part of the slogan, and we didn't either. Nor did we ask him whether he thought it was very subtle. His car was facing east. Rupert and I walked with him to the roadside, thanked him for his help, and he continued on his way. We went and gathered all the tools together before taking a final glance at the statue.

'Look,' I said. 'He's forgotten his rope.'

It was still hanging over Baroness Turnpike's left arm.

'He must have been distracted,' said Rupert. 'Never mind. He can pick it up when he comes through next week.'

Now that the job was done I began to

wonder if it had been worth it. After all, the school remained in a state of disrepair, the lawn looked as though it had been ploughed up, and the hedge was in serious need of attention.

'In reality,' I said, 'we've barely made a difference.'

'We've done what we can,' said Rupert, 'which is all we can do.'

We emerged onto the road just as a car came rolling along from the east. When the driver drew level with us he slowed down and wound open his window.

'Wanna ride?' he called.

He didn't stop though.

By the time we got back to the gatehouse the light was beginning to fade. We carefully placed the tools in the back of Martin's van, exactly where we'd found them, then we went and finished off his cake.

11.

Great Britain may have been a national park, but it was hardly an idyll of boundless greenery. The process of afforestation was slow and steady, and there were still thousands of unoccupied homes, shops, offices, schools and factories yet to be wholly absorbed into the encroaching vegetation. Moreover, there were some properties that had been brand new or under construction at the time of the purchase. Made from robust modern materials, they offered substantial resistance to the relentless onslaughts of nature. Immense monoliths of glass refused to submit to the thriving woodlands that lapped against them; reinforced concrete yielded only reluctantly; steel girders rebuffed the leafy deluge.

Rupert and I noted all this as we headed towards the MovieDrome a few days later. Everywhere we looked we saw cranes, signal gantries, gas-holders, wind turbines, communication masts and pylons sticking up above the trees. Most of them were now surplus to requirements, but they were plainly going to be around for a good few years yet.

'Ironic really,' said Rupert. 'People used to regard pylons as blights on the landscape, but nowadays the sight of them makes me feel quite nostalgic.'

It was late in the afternoon. Three unfinished skyscrapers soared high above a building site we were passing. Dotted around them were several redundant tower cranes that stood immobile and gaunt, their jibs stowed vertically. The name of the construction company, painted white on a bright blue background, was gradually peeling off. A flock of birds circled slowly above. Something had attracted their interest, though we couldn't make out what exactly. The crane nearest to us was a little taller than the others, and as we peered upwards there was a sudden flash of sunlight on the driver's cabin. It was hardly anything, a brief glimmer that only lasted an instant, but we both noticed it.

'See that?' said Rupert. 'The cabin door must be swinging in the breeze.'

'But there's scarcely a breath of wind today,' I countered.

'Down here, no,' he said, 'but it could be very different up there.'

As if to confirm his argument, the birds wheeled lazily away to the south, seemingly without flapping their wings. Soon they were lost from view. We were about to continue our journey when a second flash of sunlight stopped us in our tracks.

'That door's not swinging in the wind,' I said. 'Somebody's opening and closing it.'

Sure enough, after a few more seconds we saw the tiny figure of a man emerge from the cabin, close the door behind him, then step onto an adjacent platform. This appeared to have a safety rail around it. The man moved to the far side of the platform and remained there for about half a minute before going back inside the cabin.

'Bet I can guess who that is,' said Rupert.

'Carruthers?' I suggested.

'Must be him,' he said. 'He obviously enjoys clambering around at great heights.'

Once more the man emerged from the cabin and closed the door, but this time, instead of stepping onto the platform, he swung onto the top rung of a ladder and began making a careful descent. It was a long way down and it would take him a while to reach the ground.

'I don't think he just climbs about for the sake of it,' I said. 'I reckon he's conducting some kind of survey.'

'Possibly,' said Rupert. 'He's always on the move, isn't he? Perhaps he's searching for a better perspective.'

'Quite.'

We watched as Carruthers continued down

the ladder. He looked very confident, as though he'd performed the feat many times before, and when he reached halfway we saw that he was carrying a pair of binoculars suspended on a strap over his shoulder.

'He's never without them,' observed Rupert. 'Seem to be the tools of his trade.'

'And his bunch of keys,' I added. 'He probably had to unlock that cabin to get in.'

The perimeter of the building site was lined with huge timber hoardings which obscured our view of Carruthers as he neared the foot of the ladder. We knew, however, that there was an entrance at the corner, so we wandered towards it with the vague idea of saying 'hello' to him. The ground at the entrance was covered in a thick layer of mud, baked hard after several weeks of sunshine, and deeply rutted by the inroads of countless dumper trucks which had long since departed. Beyond the mud, the site had been colonised by assorted grasses, nettles and thistles that grew almost waist-high. We couldn't see Carruthers, but the ladder was empty so we knew he'd got down safely.

'Where's he gone then?' said Rupert.

Next moment we heard a car engine start up and a black sedan came nosing round from behind the crane, flattening a clump of nettles as it headed towards the entrance. Carruthers was at the wheel but he failed to see us as he concentrated on getting the vehicle across the ruts. As it was, he managed to scrape its bottom on the dried mud, throwing up a large cloud of dust before finally getting clear. When he reached the road he set off in the direction of the MovieDrome.

'That's a shame,' I remarked. 'He could have given us a lift.'

'Not really,' said Rupert. 'Don't forget we'll be turning off before we get there to check out those guys at the other gate.'

'Oh, yes,' I said. 'Of course.'

'Besides,' he added, 'we don't want

Carruthers knowing everything we're doing, do we?'

I looked at Rupert with surprise.

'Surely you don't still think he's spying on us,' I said. 'I thought we ruled that out weeks ago.'

'Not spying, no,' replied Rupert. 'Let's just say he's a little too inquisitive for my liking.'

He didn't elaborate further, so we then resumed our journey.

This question of 'checking out the guys at the other gate' was bothering me slightly. After all, we wouldn't be visiting in any official capacity (we didn't even have a van with PARK AUTHORITY emblazoned along its sides) and I wondered how Rupert intended to approach the matter. Hopefully we weren't simply going to turn up and demand to know the reason they were opening and closing the gate (which may have been inconvenient to motorists but was hardly illegal). In my opinion a degree of subtly would work better. I suggested to Rupert that we should appear at the gate in the manner of innocents abroad and casually play along with their line of enquiry. Maybe ask a few naive questions of our own. By such methods we could probably deduce what exactly they were trying to find out. Rupert's response was merely to say that we'd wait and see what happened.

Evening was now drawing near. The main purpose of our excursion was to see if there was a film showing at the MovieDrome, so we planned to arrive there after nightfall. We'd timed it pretty well, though, and there were still twenty minutes of daylight remaining when we reached the minor road that led to the other gate.

'Just a diversion,' Rupert assured me. 'Won't take long.'

In the past we'd become fairly familiar with this road because it provided a useful alternative route to the MovieDrome when traffic on the main road was heavy. These days, of course, heavy traffic was unheard of. As a matter of fact we'd barely seen any vehicles since Carruthers drove away an hour earlier. A few cars had passed us heading towards the coast, but now that we'd turned off there were none at all. It occurred to me that the two guys at the gate needed to be exceedingly patient. Their enquiries must have been very important to make them hang around all day long the way they did.

'If only we knew what they were looking for,' I said, 'then we might be able to help them.'

'Or perhaps not,' said Rupert. 'Look.'

He was pointing at two black sedans parked at the roadside about fifty yards ahead of us. Even from this distance we could see that one of them was covered in a layer of dust. Beyond them was the gate, which was closed. Beside it stood three men, deep in conversation.

I felt a restraining hand on my arm. Rupert put his finger to his lips and indicated an abandoned phonebox. Swiftly the two of us stepped behind it.

'Do you think they noticed us?' he asked.

'Probably not,' I replied. 'They're too busy talking.'

'Well, we'll just stay here for a while and keep an eye on them.'

'Now who's spying?'

Rupert ignored my accusation and peeped around the corner of the phonebox.

'That's definitely Carruthers,' he said. 'To judge from the body language he's in charge of the other two. Ah, now they're opening the gate. Must be finished for the day.'

Any minute we expected to hear the sound of car engines starting. Instead, there was only silence. Eventually Rupert looked again.

'They're heading up the road,' he said. 'They've gone quite a long way already.'

There was a note of urgency in his voice that I'd never heard before. I followed his gaze and could just make out the three men in the distance. To my surprise I saw that they were all jogging along, shoulder to shoulder, in a tightknit group.

'Maybe that's our mystery training squad,' I ventured.

'I wouldn't call three a squad,' Rupert replied.

'There might be others joining them along the way.'

'Well, let's see shall we? They're not going particularly fast. Let's get after them.'

12.

The three men were obviously following the road around towards the MovieDrome. Rupert and I set off at a gentle pace, keeping them in sight but taking care not to get too close. Fortunately they never thought of looking behind them. Moreover, the light was failing rapidly. There was a very long curve ahead of us, then a junction where the men turned right onto a straight, narrow road.

They jogged so slowly that we were now in danger of catching up with them. For a moment we were tempted to overtake them to show that we were faster, but we managed to resist the urge. We could now see the MovieDrome looming up ahead of us. Before that the road widened briefly at the point where the buses used to turn around. Here the men came to a sudden halt, apparently to catch their breath.

'All their talk about working the British until they melt,' said Rupert. 'They ought to sort themselves out first.'

After a brief pause the men continued at ordinary walking speed. They looked small beside the high fence that surrounded the MovieDrome. This had been designed in such a way that passers-by would be unable to see the film that was being shown. We knew that the main entrance was further along the road. Nearby, however, was a service door which the three men now approached. We watched as Carruthers produced his bunch of keys, unlocked the door and ushered his two companions inside. He went in last, closing the door behind him.

Rupert and I allowed a couple of minutes to pass before strolling over and cautiously trying the door. It was locked. We walked along to the main entrance, which was closed and blocked with concrete barriers. We then followed the perimeter fence all the way around, looking for other ways in, but there were none. We stood outside the MovieDrome and waited as darkness fell.

Shortly afterwards we became aware of a flickering in the sky immediately overhead. We could also hear a soundtrack which, despite being muffled by the high fence, we recognised at once. There was the familiar theme tune that always went with the newsreels, together with an effusive commentary. Now we were certain beyond doubt that it was the film about Lee Montana. The voice-over portrayed her as a star in the making and bewailed the loss of her untapped talent, destined never to be enjoyed by a disappointed public. Rupert and I had seen the newsreel on numerous occasions. As we listened, we could easily picture Lee Montana riding her elephant bareback through the savannah, accompanied by some ostriches, some zebra, and a young giraffe.

Nonetheless, we were at a loss to explain why the men in the MovieDrome kept watching it over and over again. After it finished there was a slight delay before the film started once more from the beginning. By now we practically knew the soundtrack by heart. When it was repeated for a third time we decided to head for home.

There was no street lighting so we went via the main road. As we walked we began to discuss Lee Montana.

'You know when she went missing,' I said. 'Did they send out any search parties?'

'Presumably,' replied Rupert.

'There was no mention of them in the newsreel.'

'No, I suppose there wasn't, come to think of it.'

'You'd think it would be easy to find an elephant.'

'Maybe so, but they must have known they were wasting their time.'

'How do you mean?'

'Well, have you ever seen an African elephant? They're massive with huge, great tusks.

You can't catch them, let alone tame them. You definitely can't ride them.'

'So why did the film company choose Africa?'

'They were plainly misinformed,' said Rupert. 'All the tame elephants come from India.'

'So they should have gone there instead?'

'Possibly,' he conceded, 'but they didn't really need to go as far as that.'

Briefly I reflected on his words.

'Surely, you're not suggesting…?'

'I'm suggesting nothing,' he said, 'but it's often struck me as a bit odd the way the background scenery in the newsreel is all blurry. She's supposed to be riding her elephant through the savannah, but actually she could be anywhere.'

'I thought that was intentional,' I said, 'to lend a degree of mystique to the story.'

'Oh, yes, it's intentional alright,' Rupert replied, 'but I don't think it's got anything to do with mystique.'

For a while we were occupied with our own thoughts. We walked on without talking, and gradually I realized that the theme from the newsreel was still going round and round in my head. It had been stuck there ever since we left the MovieDrome, and now I simply couldn't get rid of it. I should add, though, that the tune was far from dull. Quite the opposite in fact. The film company seemed to have plundered it from a famous classical work (lots of sweeping strings, stirring brass, crashing drums and so forth). They'd also taken the liberty of speeding it up a bit. The result was an anthem of majestic splendour. Vaguely I wondered what the composer would have thought if he'd known that his masterpiece would be used years later as theme music for the exploits of a girl on an elephant. Perhaps he wouldn't have minded.

The moon was now rising to guide us home. It had been a long walk and we were looking forward to getting back. All was quiet. Traffic on the road was as sparse as we would have expected at this late hour and we hardly saw any vehicles. When we were about half a mile from our gate, however, we were overtaken by a car travelling towards the park. We watched its tail-lights fading into the distance, but then all of a sudden it braked and they flared up bright red. Next moment we saw the flash of the car's headlights as it carried out a three-point turn. Shortly afterwards it passed us going the other way and rapidly disappeared into the night.

'Wherever he planned to go,' remarked Rupert, 'he must have changed his mind.'

This seemed the likely reason for the about-turn, but we soon discovered we were wrong. As we drew near the gate we saw that it was no longer open, which was how we'd left it several hours earlier. There was also a sign, newly-attached, and in the moonlight we read the words:

GATE CLOSED FOR PAINTING

13.

'Martin must have been here,' I said. 'Bit of a funny time to pay a visit.'

'Well, we can't leave the gate closed all night,' said Rupert. 'Otherwise we'll be woken by a constant stream of cars turning round.'

I wasn't sure about a 'constant stream' (it would be half a dozen at the most) but broadly I agreed with Rupert. We guessed that the painters would appear sometime the following morning. Therefore, we decided to leave the gate open overnight.

'We'll just have to get up early and close it before they arrive,' concluded Rupert.

He reached for the gate to swing it back in the usual manner, but it refused to move.

'Don't tell me it's locked,' he said.

Closer examination proved that the gate was indeed locked. We checked inside the gatehouse in case somebody had left a key, but there was none. Neither was there any kind of note or message.

'That's rather high-handed,' I said. 'Locking the gate without so much as a "by your leave".'

'Inexcusable,' said Rupert.

Our disgruntlement was further compounded when we considered the disruption this would inevitably cause. If the gate was going to be painted then traffic would need to be diverted elsewhere, which would clearly involve the two of us having to give directions to all and sundry. Ahead of us lay a disturbed night with cars liable to turn up at any time, and furthermore we would have to rise early the next morning to greet the painters.

'I bet you wish you hadn't mentioned it needed painting,' I said.

Rupert ignored my comment and headed for his bunk bed.

'Expect they'll be here about eight o'clock,' he announced, 'so we'll have to be ready for them.'

I slept very badly. In normal circumstances, if a vehicle happened to go by in the dead of night, it would slow down to pass through the gateway, its engine would give a gentle roar as it accelerated, and then it would be gone. We were so accustomed to these sounds that they seldom interrupted our sleep. With the gate closed, by contrast, I found myself lying awake, expecting the silence to be broken at any moment. In the event, I counted only two more cars during the remaining hours of darkness, and they weren't particularly noisy when they turned around. Nevertheless, when daylight came I felt completely shattered. The same went for Rupert. We skirted each other bad-temperedly as we had our breakfast, and then we began waiting for the painters to show up.

'I suppose Martin must have got his van

repaired,' I said at length.

'Well, whoever fixed it was a quick worker,' replied Rupert. 'Don't forget his clutch had gone. That's more than a half-hour job.'

'Maybe they towed it away.'

'Yes, maybe.'

Eventually we went round to the back of the gatehouse to have a look, and were astonished to see Martin's van in the same place it had been for the last couple of weeks. It was now engulfed in a dense clump of nettles.

'Nobody's been anywhere near that van,' declared Rupert, 'let alone mended it.'

'So how did he get here?'

'You tell me.'

Our conversation had to be postponed because the first vehicles of the day were beginning to arrive. The sign on the gate informed drivers of the reason for the closure, but this didn't stop them winding down their windows and enquiring how long the job would take. It was a question we were unable to answer, and we could see that some of them thought we were being unhelpful.

'I'll be glad when those painters get started,' I said, as yet another dissatisfied motorist pulled away.

'Well, if they don't get here soon,' said Rupert, 'they'll have lost half the morning.'

It was ten o'clock and the weather was fair. Perfect painting conditions, I would have thought, but still they failed to appear. As the hours ticked slowly by we found ourselves subsiding into a sort of limbo. There was nothing we could do really except hang around waiting for the painters. Cars came and went. We had lunch. The afternoon drifted along. About four-thirty, for no apparent reason, Rupert wandered over to inspect the sign more closely.

'Have you noticed,' he said, 'that it's completely different to the sign Martin made for the gap in the hedge?'

'I hadn't noticed, no,' I replied.

'Well, it's black and white instead of red and white, and the lettering is quite bland.'

'Yes, I see what you mean.'

'Martin's letters are more artistic.'

'Perhaps somebody else made it,' I suggested.

'Possibly,' said Rupert, 'but you'd think the park authority would have an official style which they'd always adhere to.'

'The lettering on the side of his van is quite artistic,' I pointed out.

'Oh, yes, it is, isn't it?'

My observation seemed to satisfy Rupert for the time being, though he was still obviously frustrated by the current state of affairs. He rattled the gate. The lock remained secure.

This more or less set the pattern for the next few days. Each morning we rose early from our beds in the hopeful expectation of welcoming the painters, and each morning we were disappointed. Ahead of us lay many fruitless hours. The only consolation was the fact that there were now hardly any vehicles turning up. We soon gathered that the majority of drivers had taken to using the other gate near the MovieDrome, even though they faced being stopped and questioned by the guys with the black sedan, Every evening we witnessed the flickering in the sky as the newsreel about Lee Montana was shown yet again.

Around noon on Wednesday a familiar car stopped outside the gatehouse. Behind the wheel sat Ambrose. He peered through his windscreen at the sign about the closure, then got out and strolled over to speak to us.

'I heard you were closed,' he said, 'but I had to drop by this way to collect my coil of rope.'

'Ah, yes,' said Rupert. 'It's still hanging where you left it.'

'You mean on the statue?'

'Yes.'

'But I thought you'd have put it somewhere for safekeeping.'

'Sorry, no,' I said. 'We didn't.'

Ambrose shook his head with dismay, as though to suggest we'd somehow neglected our duties.

'So it's still there, is it?' he asked.

'Should be.'

The western gate was only closed to road traffic. Pedestrians could pass it on either side, so without a further word Ambrose set off on foot towards the Turnpike Senior School for Girls.

'I think that's put him in a bad mood,' I remarked.

'Can't be helped,' said Rupert. 'It's not our job to look after people's ropes. He shouldn't have been so careless. It's not as if he's a friend of ours or anything. He only comes through once a week.'

Rupert and I watched as Ambrose slipped through the gap in the raggedy hedge. Any minute we expected him to emerge again carrying his coil of rope. Instead he reappeared empty-handed and beckoned us to join him.

'Oh, now what?' murmured Rupert.

With nothing better to do, we walked up to where Ambrose was waiting.

'Something the matter?' I enquired.

'Take a look for yourself.'

We gazed across the school lawn and saw the statue of Baroness Turnpike lying flat on the ground, face down. A closer examination showed that this time she'd been pulled over rather than pushed.

She was now several yards from her original position.

'They must have used your rope,' said Rupert.

'Probably,' said Ambrose. 'This wouldn't have happened if you'd put it somewhere safe.'

'Well, you shouldn't have left it hanging around.'

I sensed there was a squabble brewing

between the two of them, which I really would have preferred to avoid. Initially I'd assumed Ambrose was of the same ilk as Carruthers and company, perpetually interfering in the running of the park, but I was coming to see that he was merely pursuing a gentlemanly interest, whereas they tended to act like paid officials. In the absence of proper officials (Martin, for example) they seemed to be taking over the park for their own purposes. In view of this, I felt it would be better to embrace Ambrose as an ally rather than fall out with him. I knew I had to act fast.

'Right,' I said briskly, 'we'd better see about getting the Baroness stood up again.'

My suggestion had the desired calming effect on Ambrose and Rupert. For the next few minutes they worked closely together, studying the problem, and finally concluding it was a task beyond the three of us.

'She's been moved too far,' said Ambrose. 'It would take a whole squad of men to get her back to where she was.'

'We'll have to leave her for the time being,' concurred Rupert.

The crisis over, we conducted a brief search for Ambrose's rope. There was no trace of it, and we guessed the miscreants had taken it away with them.

'I'll just have to get another one,' said Ambrose. Absently he bent down and picked up a large feather that was lying amongst the trampled grass at his feet. He studied it for a moment, then nodded towards the hedge. 'Looks as if they've done some more damage.'

We could now see that there was a second gap in the hedge, further along the road.

'Will you be reporting that?' he asked, 'or shall I inform those fellows at the other gate?'

'We'll record it in our logbook,' I assured him.

'Good,' he said. 'It's most likely the kind of thing they're watching out for.'

With Ambrose still carrying his feather we made our way back to the gatehouse.

'Any idea what type of bird that came from?' I enquired.

'No,' said Ambrose, 'but I'll try to find out.'

He got into his car and stuck the feather in the dashboard.

'Right,' he said. 'I'll get going. I presume they'll have finished the painting by next Wednesday?'

'Hopefully,' I replied (though I had my doubts).

After he'd gone we had some lunch and then prepared ourselves for another long, listless afternoon of waiting.

14.

The absence of passers-by, even those who complained, was beginning to tell on the pair of us. Rupert, I noticed, was becoming especially irritable. Therefore, it was quite a relief when after only a few minutes we heard a vehicle approaching from the west. We both stepped out of the gatehouse, only to be confronted by the sight of Martin's van. It was being driven by Carruthers. He gave us a wave, then carefully manoeuvred it behind the gatehouse and back into its clump of nettles. We heard a door slam, and a moment later he came and joined us.

'How did you get that van moving?' I asked. 'We were told the clutch had gone.'

'Nothing wrong with it,' said Carruthers. 'Just needed some adjustment, that was all.'

'Been for a test drive?'

'Yes,' he said. 'You weren't around, so I

couldn't let you know.'

'We weren't far away.'

'You weren't around,' he repeated with a shrug.

Casually I wondered what he was doing here and why he'd taken it upon himself to 'adjust' Martin's clutch. Meanwhile, he stood back and peered admiringly at the gate.

'Fine looking structure,' he remarked.

'Yes.'

'Designed by the president's son-in-law.'

'So we gathered.'

'Actually, it's a bit of a nuisance the gate being closed all the time,' said Rupert. 'We have to keep redirecting people.'

This brought a sharp response from Carruthers.

'What's wrong?' he snapped. 'Too much like hard work?'

'Not really, but it causes a lot of inconvenience.'

Carruthers didn't seem to hear Rupert's answer. Instead, he adopted a declamatory tone, and spoke as if he was addressing a public meeting.

'The British are so damned awkward,' he announced. 'All they care about is going home early on a Friday.'

'It's got nothing to do with going home early on a Friday,' said Rupert. 'As a matter of fact this is our home.'

'So what's the problem then?'

'It's inconvenient,' I said. 'For everybody.'

Carruthers reviewed the situation for several seconds. He then reached into a pocket, produced a bunch of keys, selected one and unlocked the gate, which he swung wide open.

'Thanks,' I said. 'That's a great help.'

He nodded.

'Maybe you could return the favour,' he said. 'We need recourse to your local knowledge.'

'Oh yes?'

'There's a sports stadium we've been unable to locate. It's near here somewhere. Apparently it's shaped like an oval.'

I knew exactly where he meant.

'It's always been notoriously hard to find,' I said. 'People used to take the signs away for souvenirs.'

'Well, somebody should have stopped them,' said Carruthers. 'We've been delayed unnecessarily.'

'Why didn't you go to the mapping agency?' Rupert asked. 'That would have been the easiest solution.'

Carruthers gave him a penetrating look.

'You may not have heard' he said, 'but the mapping agency was ransacked quite recently. All the maps were mangled beyond recognition.'

'No, we hadn't heard,' said Rupert.

'I don't know how anybody got in there,' I said. 'The doors are made from solid oak.'

'The doors were simply demolished,' said Carruthers. 'Smashed to splinters.'

'Who would do such a thing?'

'We can't even guess,' he said. 'There's no obvious suspect.'

Just then a car came trundling along the road from the west. It was a large black sedan, covered with dust.

'Ah, good,' said Carruthers. 'Here's Presley.'

The car pulled up beside us, and we recognised the driver as one of the guys from the other gate. He got out and gave Rupert and me a nod each, but didn't introduce himself. Carruthers took him aside and they conferred quietly. Rupert glanced at me and disappeared into the gatehouse, closing the door behind him.

When they'd finished their consultation, Carruthers called me over.

'Are you ready to go now?' he enquired.

'To the stadium?'

'Yes'.

'Okay,' I said. 'Suppose so.'

He indicated the passenger seat of his car and I got in. Meanwhile, Presley walked round behind the gatehouse. I heard a door slam and an engine starting, and next minute Martin's van came into view. Presley gave us a wave and drove off into the west.

Once Carruthers was back behind the wheel of his own car he seemed to loosen up a little. We headed through the gate and into the park, with me giving directions when necessary, and as we proceeded his mood became positively expansive.

'Why this particular stadium?' I asked.

'Not just this one,' he said. 'We're listing all of them. We want to find every stadium, sports ground and outdoor arena in the land.'

'Is this for the physical training regime?' I said. 'To work the British hard until they melt?'

Carruthers took a few seconds to consider

the question. More than a few seconds in fact, and I got the impression he was trying to think back to our previous encounter.

'That's the idea,' he said at length. 'Kind of.'

When we finally arrived at the sports stadium I was pleased to note what good condition it was in. There was little evidence of deterioration and I felt quite proud to be showing it to a newcomer for the first time. It was a very famous stadium, and rightly so. Carruthers, however, appeared unimpressed.

'I thought it would be bigger than this,' he said.

When we got out of the car I noticed he had his binoculars with him. We wandered around the perimeter and looked at the numerous entrances equipped with brightly painted turnstiles. All of them were barred by tubular steel gates, and all of them were locked, but it came as no surprise when Carruthers produced a key that fitted. We went inside and stood on the grass, now overgrown, gazing at row upon row of seats rising high above us.

'Wait here,' said Carruthers abruptly.

He set off towards one of the gangways that ran between the seats and began climbing up the steep concrete steps. This was the first time I'd been in this stadium for many years and I had no intention of waiting just because Carruthers said so. Instead I headed for the opposite gangway and made my way to the very top. The view from the upper seats had a reputation for being unsurpassed. Not only could spectators enjoy all the action within the stadium: they could also see for miles outside as well. Over on the opposite stairway, Carruthers had already reached the summit and was now peering through his binoculars into the hinterland beyond. He was looking northward, while I had a full panorama of the south.

There before me lay countless buildings,

railway stations, bus garages, brick works, colleges and libraries, all of them being gradually enveloped by dense vegetation. It was now late afternoon, almost dusk actually, and as I gazed into the distance I thought I saw a slight movement about a mile away. I blinked in the twilight and looked again. There was a short stretch of grassland punctuated with shrubs, possibly the remnants of a public garden, and crossing from one side to the other I saw a girl riding on an elephant, accompanied by some ostriches, some zebra and a young giraffe.

15.

It was dark when Carruthers dropped me off at the gatehouse. He'd barely uttered a word on the entire journey home and had gunned his car hard and fast along the uneven roads, bouncing over sporadic humps and potholes, the headlights blazing on full beam. He was plainly displeased with me. We'd lost each other for a while in the deepening gloom of the stadium and for some reason he thought it was my fault. In my opinion it was due simply to mischance. I'd decided to walk around the upper rim to the point where I'd last seen him at the top of the concrete stairway, but by the time I got there he'd vanished. After waiting a few minutes I descended to ground level, expecting to find him back where we started, yet there was still no sign of him. For a moment I had visions of him locking the gate and leaving me behind. I was debating what to do next when suddenly all the stadium floodlights came on. A disembodied voice crackled over the tannoy system.

'Oh, there you are!' it said. 'Don't move!'

The floodlights went out again and after a short delay Carruthers emerged from the shadows.

'I wish you'd done as I asked you,' he murmured.

He didn't strike me as the sort of person who accepted excuses, so I said nothing by way of apology or explanation. We left the deserted stadium, locked up, and returned to his car.

Now, as we approached the gatehouse, I saw that the light bulb in the kitchen was lit. This told me Rupert was preparing supper. Carruthers pulled up and I got out.

'Well,' I said, through his open window, 'that's another stadium to add to your list.'

'Thank you,' he answered reluctantly.

Without saying goodbye he drove off into the west. I walked a few paces up the road and looked towards the distant MovieDrome. As usual there was a flickering in the sky above it. I watched for five or six minutes until the flickering ceased, then went inside for my supper.

Rupert greeted me with a nod. The table was already set, so I sat down and the two of us ate for a while in silence.

Finally Rupert spoke.

'Get there alright?' he asked.

'Yes,' I said. 'The roads were empty.'

'Carruthers satisfied?'

'Didn't seem like it. Not big enough, apparently.'

'That comes as no surprise.'

There was a further silence. I decided to change the subject. 'I've got something to ask you,' I said.

'Oh yes?'

'You know the newsreel about Lee Montana?'

'Of course.'

'And you know it's been scientifically proved that light can be bent?'

'Yes.'

'Well, do you think it's possible that somehow by accident or perhaps even deliberately the film could be projected upwards into the sky and in certain atmospheric conditions sort of deflected as if through a prism so that the images appear somewhere else about ten miles away?'

'No,' said Rupert.

'Thought not.'

He rose from his seat and went and peered through the window.

'Anyway,' he said, 'it's beginning to cloud over. We're in for some rain at long last.'

We finished supper and I did the washing up.

As the evening became darker I thought about the greenery that had flourished so rapidly during the past few weeks without the help of any rainfall. I thought of the grass growing in the roads, the mossy walls and the saplings sprouting from the roofs of buildings, and I realized that the oncoming downpour was bound to hasten the process even more.

'It's turning into a jungle out there,' I remarked.

Eventually I went to bed, but I had yet another restless night. I lay for hours in my bunk wondering if my imagination was starting to play tricks on me, and whether the solitary nature of my job as gatekeeper was taking its toll. Except that it wasn't wholly solitary, was it? There were two of us, me and Rupert, and he remained as normal as ever. So maybe it wasn't my imagination, after all. Around dawn I heard the first drops of rain on the window. By now a breeze had begun to stir and the panes were rattling. To judge from the sound of it we were in for a proper deluge. I turned over and managed to fall asleep at just about the hour I should have been getting up.

16.

I was woken by a horn hooting outside. When I opened my eyes I saw Rupert padding around the room barefooted.

'Why are they hooting?' he demanded. 'The gate's wide open.'

I swung out of bed and went to the window. It was broad daylight but the rain was hammering down. There were puddles lying everywhere. Opposite the gatehouse was a large van with the words PARK AUTHORITY (PAINTING DEPARTMENT) emblazoned along the side panels. The engine was running and the windscreen wipers were hard at work. Three men were sitting in the front. Two of them wore white painter's overalls. The third man sat between them. It was Martin and he looked rather forlorn.

From my viewpoint at the window it seemed as if there was some kind of disagreement occurring within the van. The two painters appeared to be browbeating Martin over some matter, even though he was supposed to be in charge of them. He in turn was holding his hands palms upwards in a gesture of exasperation, or perhaps helplessness, or possibly resignation. I guessed the dispute must be to do with painting the gate. It was evident to me that the weather conditions made the job impossible, which surely meant there was nothing to argue about, yet still the wrangling continued.

'Come away from the window,' said Rupert. 'Leave them to it.'

We had our breakfast, then I waited half an hour before peeping out again. The van's engine had now stopped and the windscreen wipers were at rest. Condensation was misting up the windows, but I vaguely made out the three men sitting jammed together as the rain drummed down on their roof. Poor Martin! I felt sorry for him because there was no obvious way he could escape confinement, squeezed as he was between his two antagonists. If he made a dash for it he'd be soaking wet before he got halfway to the gatehouse.

In the event, however, that was precisely what he did. There was a momentary lull in the rainfall as the wind shifted slightly. In the same instant the driver's door opened, a painter got out, followed by Martin, who stood aside while the painter got in again and slammed the door shut. As quickly as it had stopped the rain resumed, though now even heavier than before. Martin took a second or two to get his bearings, then charged across to our doorway with his head down. Rupert got the door open just in time and Martin shot inside. He was now thoroughly drenched. He stood there dripping raindrops onto the floor and I noticed that his suntan had faded considerably.

'What a carry on I've had with those two,' he announced. 'They said I should have come in my own van and when I told them the clutch had gone they refused to listen. They said there wasn't room in their van for three people.'

'Looks big enough to me,' said Rupert.

'That's what I'd have thought,' said Martin, 'but they insisted the middle seat wasn't for people to sit in.'

'What's it for then?' I asked.

'According to them it's supposed to be for their sandwich boxes and their thermos flasks. They said it was their entitlement and they got themselves highly upset about it.'

I peered out of the window. Across the road I could see the two painters sitting in their van looking quite contented. Both of them were drinking from steaming thermos flasks.

'That all seems to be resolved now,' I ventured.

'Yes,' said Martin, 'and I've told them they might as well go home because they won't get any painting done today.'

'Far too wet and windy.'

'Yes.'

'Looks as if it could rain all week,' said Rupert.

'If it rains it rains,' Martin replied. 'They'll just have to come back when it's dry again.'

Outside we heard the van's engine starting up. A quick glance through the window told me that the thermos flasks had now been put away. There was a crunch of gears and the van reversed into the first part of a three-point turn.

'By the way,' said Martin, 'did somebody come and replace my clutch?'

'No,' I answered. 'Apparently it only needed adjusting.'

The painter's van completed the second part of its three-point turn.

'But it's all fixed is it?' he enquired.

'Yes,' I said, 'but it's not here any more.'

A look of consternation crossed Martin's face, as disbelief combined with suppressed panic.

'Where is it then?'

'We don't know,' said Rupert. 'Somebody called Presley drove it away.'

'Oh no!'

Martin sprang towards the door and threw it open just as the painter's van finished its manoeuvre and set off towards the west. He ran out into the road and waved his arms up and down, but to no avail. The van receded into the murky distance.

Martin returned to the shelter of our doorway.

'Sorry about that,' I said, 'but Presley acted as though he had a perfect right to drive your van.'

'Well, he did and he didn't,' said Martin. 'I've been instructed to allow him and his colleagues a completely free rein, but to tell the truth they're beginning to take a lot of liberties.'

'Who are they then?'

'I'm not permitted to say.'

'And because of them you're stuck here.'

'Yes.'

While we were on the subject of vans, I took the opportunity to raise a related matter.

'Any news about our vehicle?'

'I'm afraid not,' said Martin. 'As far as I know it's still in dock.'

He asked if he could use the guest room to go and dry off, and naturally we agreed.

'Looks like he's going to be with us for a few days,' said Rupert quietly.

'Yes,' I said. 'We'll just have to make the best of it.'

In this disorderly manner we began our working day, though it could scarcely be described as work at all. The rain kept on falling, so there was no question of going outside. Normally in wet weather we merely waved to passing cars through the window, but with Martin present we felt we really ought to try and do a little more. Our solution was to take turns standing in the open doorway, protected from the rain but still visibly 'on duty'. Martin seemed to approve of the practise and even offered to take an occasional turn himself.

Despite the rain, the flow of traffic was marginally heavier than usual, and as the hours went by we all noticed a very slight increase in the number of older models on the road. It was hardly anything, barely discernible, but it was just enough to arouse our interest.

'I wonder where they've all come from?' I pondered aloud. 'I'd always assumed most of them were obsolete.'

Martin thought he knew the answer.

'Probably got them from the MovieDrome,' he said. 'Someone repaired all those abandoned cars and auctioned them off.'

'When?'

'Last week.'

'But they were supposed to have run out of spare parts,' said Rupert, plainly astonished.

'Whoever it was must have been very

enterprising,' said Martin. 'They sold the whole lot. The place is entirely empty now.'

Just as he spoke, a car of a type I hadn't seen for years went trundling past the window.

'Look,' I said. 'Some proud new owner taking it for a spin.'

'Evidently the shortage of spare parts wasn't quite as bad as it was made out to be,' remarked Rupert. 'I was under the impression everything had to be imported these days.'

'Most things are,' said Martin. 'We even had to import the paint for the gate.'

'Is that why there was such a long delay?' I enquired.

'No,' he replied. 'It was because the painter's van wasn't mended until yesterday.'

Being reminded of the painters and their van appeared to put Martin in a sombre mood. He fell silent for a while, moping around the gatehouse and getting under our feet. He cheered up considerably when we shared our lunch with him, but actually the situation put a strain on all three of us. The chief difficulty for Rupert and me was that we didn't know how long he was going to be there. We had no idea of his intentions, yet patently he wasn't going anywhere until the rain stopped. This was an unknown quantity, but Rupert's prediction that it would last all week proved to be not far off the mark. In the event it bucketed down for three days with hardly a break. Admittedly, Martin tried to make himself as useful as possible during that time, but really there was very little that needed doing. In consequence we all felt a surge of relief when, on the third evening, the rain began to ease at last. Gradually it stopped lashing against the windows, the drainpipes ceased gurgling, and the gutters no longer dripped. The night was still cloudy and dark, but we could tell the worst was over.

By now it was getting very near bedtime. Martin was just about to head for the guest room when there was a gentle knock on the door.

'I'll answer it,' he said.

Rupert and I glanced at one another in surprise. We rarely received visitors at the gatehouse, especially at this late hour, and we hadn't heard a car pulling up. We were both at a loss to think who it could be.

We listened as Martin spoke in hushed tones to someone outside, then he closed the door and came and rejoined us. In his hand he was holding a coil of rope.

I thought he wore a rather dreamy expression.

'Who was it?' I asked.

'A young woman,' he replied. 'She didn't give her name, but she wanted to return this rope. She said you knew who it belonged to.'

'Yes, we do,' said Rupert, taking the coil and hanging it over the back of a chair.

'Oddly enough,' Martin continued, 'her face seemed familiar. I'm sure I've seen her before somewhere.'

'What was she like?'

'Very striking,' he said. 'I suppose you could best describe her as an 'outdoor girl'.'

Rupert went to the window and peered into the blackness.

'Rather late to be roaming around on her own,' he said. 'Unless, of course, she wasn't on her own.'

'Oh, there was a message as well,' said Martin suddenly. 'She said she was sorry about Baroness Turnpike because it wasn't really her fault. I'm not sure what she meant by that.'

'No,' I said. 'Me neither.'

I thought it wise to avoid further discussion about who the young woman might be, so after a lot of yawning I went to bed, hoping the others would follow suit, which they eventually did. When all the lights had been switched off I lay in my bunk listening intently for unusual noises. I'm not sure what exactly I was expecting to hear, but there wasn't a sound anyway.

17.

At first light I got up quietly, dressed, and went outside. It was a cold, damp morning and the ground was still soft from the days of rain. I walked slowly along the road towards the Turnpike Senior School for Girls, examining a trail of hoof marks that ran along the grassy verge. As I did so I had a peculiar feeling that I was being watched from afar, but when I looked around I could see nobody. After a while, however, I noticed Rupert emerging from the gatehouse. I waited as he came along to join me.

'Morning,' he said, nodding at the hoof marks. 'Quite big, some of them, aren't they?'

'Yes,' I said, indicating a parallel trail of toe prints. 'Quite a variety too.'

'Indeed.'

'What's Martin doing?'

'He's just got out of bed,' said Rupert. 'I

heard him moving about.'

'Shall we mention this to him?'

'Probably not.'

Just then we heard a voice calling from the gatehouse door as Martin wished us both a good morning. We hurried back to meet him. Fortunately his attention had been caught by the sign that said the gate was closed for painting (even though it was open).

'Did you put that there?' he enquired.

'No,' said Rupert. 'We assumed you did.'

'Oh no,' said Martin. 'It's not one of our signs.'

'Ah.'

'Besides which,' he continued, 'the gate doesn't need to be closed for painting. It can be painted whether it's open or shut.'

He spent the next few minutes removing the sign, while Rupert went inside to prepare breakfast. In the meantime I gazed into the west, wondering if and when the painters would return.

By lunchtime I'd begun to accept that today wouldn't be the day. I also realized that now the weather had improved Martin was bound to start nosing around in the vicinity. He might even decide to stroll along to the Turnpike Senior School for Girls. In which case he could hardly avoid noticing the trail of hoof prints. This in turn could lead to all kinds of enquiries.

Therefore I have to confess I was quite pleased to see Carruthers. He arrived around mid-afternoon behind the wheel of Martin's van, followed closely by Presley, who was driving ours. They pulled up and got out of the shining vehicles, apparently newly-polished.

'There you are,' Carruthers announced. 'Both fully serviced and ready to go.'

He strode around the vans in the manner of a salesman, handing the respective keys to Martin and Rupert.

'You'll be needing them soon,' he added. 'We're almost ready to begin the big round-up.'

Rupert and I hadn't seen our van for many months and we welcomed it like a long lost friend. Martin, by contrast, appeared somewhat put out. The dreamy expression he'd been wearing for most of the day was swiftly replaced by a look of wariness verging on mistrust. He walked around his van, kicking the tyres before getting into the driving seat and making a big show of adjusting all the mirrors to his personal requirements.

In the meantime a large black sedan drew up, driven by the third man we'd seen at the gate near the MovieDrome. The car no longer had a covering of dust and was now sparkling clean. The man got out and handed the keys to Carruthers. He didn't introduce himself to us.

Martin completed his adjustments and came to speak to Rupert and me, blatantly ignoring the three newcomers.

'Right,' he said. 'I'll get going at once. The painters should be here in a day or two.'

He returned to his van and drove off.

I peered at Carruthers and his companions, who all seemed rather full of themselves. The afternoon had turned sunny and they were now lounging around the black sedan, with all four doors wide open.

I walked over to them.

'Tell me,' I said. 'How exactly do you intend to 'round up' a girl on an elephant, some ostriches, some zebra and a young giraffe?'

To my surprise the three of them broke into uproarious laughter. They took several seconds to recover.

'Sounds to me,' said Carruthers, wiping tears from his eyes. 'Sounds to me as if you've been watching too many movies!'

18.

Bright and early one morning the painters arrived. They parked their van unobtrusively at the side of the road so that it wouldn't cause an obstruction, then they started preparing for work. All their cleaning equipment, pots and brushes were laid out on a handy portable workbench; a plank was placed between two small step-ladders to create a platform to stand on; and a polite notice was positioned nearby requesting passing vehicles to slow down a little. By eight o'clock they'd begun painting the gate. They paused briefly from their labours at ten when they stopped to consume the contents of their sandwich boxes and thermos flasks. Work resumed at ten-fifteen and by one o'clock the job was done.

It was a Friday.

We watched as the painter's van gave a cheerful toot before speeding away.

'There you are,' I said. 'The British are quite capable of working swiftly and efficiently when it suits them.'

'I quite agree,' replied Rupert. 'Unfortunately it doesn't suit them most of the time, which is why the president had to bail us out.'

We went and inspected their workmanship. There were no runs or omissions; not a drop of paint had been spilt or otherwise wasted. In short, they'd made an excellent job of it.

'They got their early finish,' I observed. 'How do you think they'll spend the rest of the day?'

'I expect they'll go sunbathing.'

The sight of the gleaming gate put Rupert in a reflective mood.

'Do you remember,' he said, 'around the time of the purchase when certain people raised objections?'

'I have a vague recollection,' I replied.

'Didn't they put forward an alternative plan?'

'Well, it was scarcely a plan,' said Rupert. 'It was more of a declaration. They insisted that nobody had the right to sell off the British Isles and they announced their intention to occupy part of it themselves.'

'Oh, that's right,' I said. 'The independent settlement.'

'Correct.'

Rupert signalled me to follow him into the gatehouse. He then opened a cupboard draw, from which he produced a map.

'I borrowed this from the mapping agency,' he explained. 'I was curious to know precisely where the settlement was going to be.'

It was a map of the midland counties. Rupert spread it out on the kitchen table.

'Somewhere here,' he said, perusing the map, 'is a forgotten oasis.'

'Really?'

'Figuratively speaking, of course.'

He plainly hadn't looked at the map for a while, and for a few moments he stared at it blankly.

I pointed to an area that had been shaded with pastel crayons.

'Is that it?' I asked.

'Ah, yes,' said Rupert. 'Well done.'

The place indicated was a rural district surrounded by industrial conurbation. Fairly modest in size, it abounded with pastures, woodlands, pools and streams, all criss-crossed by footpaths and bridges.

'An oasis indeed,' I remarked.

Rupert nodded thoughtfully. 'I never found out whether the settlement got properly established. Once the purchase had gone ahead all contact was lost. Shame really.'

He gazed at the shaded area for quite some time and it seemed to me as though he was trying to memorise its location. Eventually he folded up the map and put it away.

'I should have returned it to the mapping agency long ago,' he said, 'but I never got round to it.'

'Too late now,' I said. 'Someone ransacked the entire stock.'

Rupert paused and puffed out his cheeks; then he opened the drawer and removed the map again.

'You don't suppose they were looking for this, do you?' he asked. His tone was cautious.

'They could have been,' I said, 'but it's a bit drastic destroying the whole collection in the process.'

'Depends how desperate they were to find it.'

He reopened the map and we studied it more closely. One corner had been stamped with the words MAPPING AGENCY. There was also a date that recorded when Rupert borrowed the map. It turned out to be just a few weeks before the purchase took place.

'If it's the only copy,' I said, 'then you could be right.'

'Perhaps somebody heard about the independent settlement and wanted to go there.'

'Yes, perhaps.'

Just then we heard a car pull up outside. I glanced through the window and saw that Ambrose had decided to drop by.

'What's he doing here on a Friday?' I said. 'He usually comes on a Wednesday.'

Rupert put the map away and we went to say hello to Ambrose.

'I've just been having a look at Baroness Turnpike,' he announced, by way of greeting, 'and she's still lying face down in the grass.'

'Yes,' I said. 'I suppose she must be.'

'I thought the park authority might have tried to stand her up again.'

'They've been fully apprised of her predicament,' said Rupert. 'Our supervisor's seen her for himself.'

'Well,' said Ambrose, 'at least that's a start.'

Inside his car I could see the large feather he'd found on his previous visit. It was still stuck in the dashboard.

'Anyway,' he continued. 'I've been busy researching the life of Baroness Turnpike.'

'Oh yes?'

'I've discovered that she came from a family of big game hunters. They owned estates in the tropics and from what I could gather they weren't particularly fussy about choosing their targets. Seemingly they shot anything that moved, wiping out entire herds as they went, but as a young woman she rebelled against all that and went to work as an educational reformer instead. Her life was a perpetual struggle because she believed in all kinds of worthy causes, yet ultimately she succeeded. Indeed, it was Miss Emily Turnpike who devised the three Cs: cleanliness, courtesy and conservation.'

Ambrose turned and looked back at the Senior School for Girls.

'The ornamental hedge,' he added, 'was planted in her memory.'

He was clearly dismayed by the state of the tattered hedge, the abandoned buildings and the toppled statue, and for a while he fell silent. All of a sudden, though, he brightened up. Reaching into his car he retrieved the feather from the dashboard.

'This,' he said, 'comes from a Greater Crested Grebe. It's extremely rare in these parts and it's got some highly unusual traits. Apparently it sheds its tail feathers when surprised or startled.'

'Really?' I said.

On the grass verge behind Ambrose were the recent tracks of at least four zoological species, all of them rather large, and none of them native to the British Isles. For some reason, however, he'd failed to notice them.

'Surprised or startled, eh?' said Rupert.

'Well, I don't know about being startled but most of us get surprises from time to time.'

'Suppose so,' said Ambrose vaguely.

'And we've got a surprise for you.'

Rupert dashed into the gatehouse and returned with the coil of rope.

'Here you are,' he said. 'It was handed in during the week.'

I thought Rupert was taking a bit of a gamble here. After all, Ambrose might easily start asking who'd handed it in. In the event he didn't, but I made a mental note to remind Rupert to be a bit more careful in future.

'Much obliged,' said Ambrose. 'It so happens I haven't needed to give anyone a tow just lately. There seem to be far fewer broken-down cars on the roads these days.'

He stuck the feather back in his dashboard, then took the coil of rope from Rupert and tossed it into the boot.

'Heading for the coast?' I enquired.

'Yes,' he said. 'Obviously I'll have to try and avoid all those sunbathers. As a matter of fact I might cut across by the MovieDrome and see what's happening there. You know they've sold off all those abandoned cars that it used to be full of?'

'Yes, we heard as much.'

'Just a vast empty space now. Not sure what they're planning to do with it.'

Ambrose fell silent again. He peered briefly at the newly-painted gate, then looked carefully up and down the road as if taking in every detail. He gazed at the school and beyond it to the distant reaches of the Great West Road. Finally he turned to Rupert and me.

'There's nobody else based around here, is there?' he asked.

'Not as far as we know,' I replied. 'There's just us.'

'That's what I thought,' he said, 'but oddly enough I keep getting the feeling we're being watched from afar.'

19.

The nightly flickering continued, and eventually Rupert and I decided to pay another visit to the MovieDrome. This was much easier now that we had our van back, so we set off one evening just after dark. We had to take it steady because of the poor condition of the roads, but the van bowled along as smoothly as if it was on rails.

'They've done a good job with the service,' commented Rupert, who was behind the wheel.

We both enjoyed the journey and in no time at all we were passing the construction site where the three tower cranes loomed against the blackening sky. Not long afterwards we left the main road.

As we approached the MovieDrome we saw that the entrance had been unblocked and was now standing wide open. Above it was an arch bearing the words: ASSEMBLY POINT.

Rupert slowed down a little, but then without consulting me drove straight under the arch and halted a few yards inside the entrance.

'Are we allowed in here?' I asked.

'It says 'assembly point',' he replied. 'So here we are.'

We looked around us. The hard standing which had once been full of abandoned cars was now a vast empty space, just as Ambrose had described it. Everything was in shadows apart from the movie screen at the far end, where the newsreel about Lee Montana was being shown for the umpteenth time. The voice-over and accompanying music resounded from loudspeakers mounted here and there on masts. Rupert stopped the engine and we rolled down the windows to listen. We stared at the grainy image of a girl riding an elephant through the savannah, and wondered yet again whether it really was Lee Montana.

When our eyes became accustomed to the dim surroundings we gradually realized that the MovieDrome wasn't entirely empty. Over by the perimeter fence, two large sedan cars (presumably black) were parked side-by-side, facing away from us. We waited until the newsreel ended, then we strolled across.

The soundtrack had fallen temporarily silent, but now there were other noises. As we drew near to the cars we heard a ratchet spanner being worked efficiently back and forth. There were men's voices and somebody was whistling quietly to himself. We then saw that the bonnet on one of the cars was raised. A couple of inspection lamps had been clamped above the engine and the constricted light revealed Carruthers and his companions, their faces half-hidden as they bent over some task or other. They were plainly unaware of our presence, so we paused for a moment outside the range of the inspection lamps. Carruthers murmured an instruction to Presley, who turned away and disappeared into the darkness. The whistling resumed (the tune was slightly familiar) but ceased when I deliberately scuffed my feet on the ground.

Carruthers glanced in our direction.

'Hey,' he said, straightening up and wiping his hands on a rag.

'Something wrong with the car?' I asked.

'No, of course not,' he replied, 'but a little fine adjustment never did any harm.'

The other man removed the inspection lamps before slamming the bonnet shut.

'Actually you're a day or two early,' said Carruthers, 'but feel free to have a mosey round.'

'Thanks.'

'Or perhaps you'd like to watch the movie,' he continued. 'Catch it while you can: we'll be changing the reel soon.'

Even as he spoke, the huge screen lit up and the film about Lee Montana began again.

'You must have seen this quite a few

times,' I ventured, raising my voice as the soundtrack commenced.

'Oh, we never bother watching it,' said Carruthers, likewise raising his voice, 'but we like the theme tune.'

A few moments later Presley reappeared and the three of them transferred the inspection lamps to the second car. Meanwhile, Rupert and I returned to our van and watched the newsreel in its entirety. It was just as I remembered, but now I found I was more interested in the details than I had been in the past. Soon I was counting the ostriches and zebra (there were three of each) and trying to judge the height of the young giraffe. I also attempted to study the background scenery, but to no avail. It was far too blurry. When the film finished we expected Presley to go and run it once more from the beginning, but he didn't. Carruthers and company appeared totally absorbed, tinkering under the bonnet of their car, and they didn't show the newsreel again.

Rupert started the van.

'Might as well head home,' he said.

We were just about to leave when Carruthers came stalking across to us.

'Where are you going?' he demanded.

'Well,' said Rupert, through the open window, 'you seem to have set up a nice little operation here with the cars and everything. We don't wish to disturb you any longer.'

'The cars aren't important,' said Carruthers. 'They're just a hobby. Something we do in our spare time while we're waiting to begin.'

'Begin what?'

'Rounding up the sunbathers. We thought you'd come to help.'

He spoke these words in such a matter-of-fact way that it took a few seconds for them to sink in. When they did I was dumbfounded, but fortunately Rupert managed to offer a suitable reply.

'Naturally, we don't mind helping,' he said

at length, 'but we'd need to know what it would entail.'

From my position in the passenger seat I noticed him quietly slipping the van into gear.

'Now don't be silly,' said Carruthers, who'd obviously noticed as well. 'I can assure you it's all very beneficial. If you'll just come along with me I'll be able to explain it better.'

Rupert and I peered at one another in the gloom, then he switched off the engine and we both got out.

Carruthers led us to a notice board where a large map of the British Isles was displayed. He shone a torch and we saw myriads of tiny crosses covering its length and breadth.

'I'm afraid the map's a little rudimentary,' he said. 'We had to draw it up from scratch. Each of these crosses represents a stadium, sports ground or similar outdoor arena. There are hundreds of them dotted throughout the country.'

'Yes,' I said. 'I suppose there must be.'

'And they'll make ideal dispersal points.'

'For sunbathers?'

'That's the plan.'

Carruthers clapped his hands together.

'We've got nothing against sunbathers personally,' he said, 'but the trouble is they make the beaches look untidy. They lie around in all manner of supine repose, half-naked or even less, and remain there for hours on end. The worst time is when the tide's coming in and they're all crowded together in a torpid mass of oil-soaked bodies. The president found it most unsightly.'

'So he's been here recently, has he?' enquired Rupert.

'He flew along the coast in his plane,' said Carruthers. 'He didn't trouble himself to land.'

In the past few moments we'd been joined by Presley and the other man. Each of them was carrying a metal tool box. They regarded us in silence while Carruthers resumed his exposition.

'As usual, however, the president came up

with a solution. There's no doubt he's a man of extraordinary ability. He devised the following programme. We're going to clear the beaches of sunbathers and bring them here to see a short educational film. The subject will be clarified at a later date. Afterwards we'll move them to the outdoor arenas where they can sunbathe to their heart's content. Under our supervision, of course. They'll be distributed equally, with no favouritism or special pleading.'

In the absence of a flickering newsreel, the MovieDrome felt particularly dark. I noticed the loudspeakers were making a dull humming noise. A breeze had got up during the evening and was playing at the edges of the map, causing it to ripple slightly on the notice board. Carruthers shone his torch again and we examined the places where the sunbathers would be taken.

'Well,' remarked Rupert, 'I guess it beats being melted down for lard.'

'Yes, that's what we thought too,' said

Carruthers. 'The president's solution is far more agreeable.'

'How are you planning to get them off the beaches?' I asked. 'They'll be very reluctant to leave.'

'Oh, there are plenty of incentives,' he replied. 'For example, we'll provide sunbeds at reasonable rates.'

'Nice.'

'Which is where you come in. They should really hear it from their own people to get them 'on side' as it were. For this purpose you'll be equipped with megaphones.'

Carruthers beamed earnestly at Rupert and me.

'Needless to say it won't just be you two,' he added. 'You'll be part of a large team of volunteers.'

'Right.'

The dull humming noise continued.

'Wanna cup of coffee?' said Presley.

'Er, no, thanks,' said Rupert, answering for the pair of us. 'We'll probably get going now. Thanks anyway.'

Carruthers requested that we came back on Wednesday morning to make the final arrangements. He walked with us to the van and waved us off.

'See you soon,' he said.

Presley and the other man also gave us a wave.

We headed out under the arch and towards the main road. Neither of us spoke at all for the first couple of miles. The windows were still open and we were both content to listen to the world going past outside. Eventually, though, something had to be said, and it was Rupert who said it.

'1 don't really like the idea of being part of a team,' he began. 'I've never considered myself a 'team player'.'

'No,' I affirmed. 'Nor me.'

'And it most likely falls outside the terms

of our employment.'

'Yes.'

'There's also the question of perceived misuse of a park authority vehicle.'

'Indeed.'

With the matter supposedly settled, we continued our journey. We passed the three tower cranes and were soon turning onto the Great West Road. As usual it was cloaked in darkness. We had only our headlights for guidance, and luckily Rupert was taking it easy because all at once a figure appeared in the middle of the carriageway, urgently flagging us down. It was Ambrose. Behind him was a telegraph pole, stretched across the road amidst a tangle of wires. We stopped and got out of the van. Ambrose came and joined us.

'Am I glad to see you,' he said. 'I've been stuck here for almost an hour.'

He indicated his car at the other side of the telegraph pole.

'Why's this suddenly fallen down?' I said.

'The last storm was a couple of weeks ago and that was hardly gale force.'

We examined the pole. The timber was badly decayed. Nonetheless, a great deal of force would have been required to snap it off at the base. Rupert suggested it was an act of nature. Ambrose was doubtful.

'Whatever the cause,' he said, 'we'd better get it moved.'

Apparently he'd already tried towing it away with his car but the tyres wouldn't grip. He reckoned some additional weight over the rear wheels would do the trick. Under his direction we attached the tow rope, then Rupert and I clambered onto the back of his car. The tactic worked, and gradually the pole was moved out of the way. Ambrose thanked us for our help.

'Curiously enough,' he said, 'I've seen several other telegraph poles recently that look as if they've just fallen over. Come to think of it, there were also a few bent lamp posts. Rather puzzling really.'

We helped him move aside the tangle of wires; then we wished him goodnight and left him pondering the conundrum. The rest of our journey homeward was uneventful. We passed some of the felled poles that Ambrose had mentioned, but none of them were causing blockages.

'This wave of destruction,' observed Rupert, 'suggests to me that somebody is becoming increasingly frustrated.'

We arrived at the gatehouse and parked the van round the back. I went in immediately and switched the lights on, but Rupert remained outside for a while. I wasn't sure what he was doing, but when I looked through the window I saw him pacing up and down the road deep in contemplation. He then approached the gatehouse and studied it from a range of different angles. When he noticed me behind the window he came inside.

'Tell me,' he said. 'If you were in charge

of a roving menagerie of herbivores, where would you take them?'

'Hopefully to some kind of watering hole,' I replied, 'with plenty of grazing.'

'Good thinking, but where exactly?'

'Certainly not around here. All we've got are a few public gardens with flower beds, ornamental lakes and fountains that don't work. Barely adequate, I'd have thought.'

'How about a figurative oasis?'

'Yes,' I said, 'that would be better.'

Rupert seemed satisfied with my answer and retired to bed.

In the middle of the night we heard a distant crash as yet another telegraph pole was brought down.

20.

The following day a park authority van arrived at the gatehouse. It was driven by Martin and once again he wore his hunted look.

'Morning,' he said, when we went out to greet him. 'I expect you know about this plan to round up all the sunbathers?'

'Yes,' I said, 'we've got an inkling.'

'I'm not too keen on the idea myself,' he confided, 'but I suppose we'll have to comply.'

He opened the back of his van and produced a megaphone and a set of sealed instructions, which he handed to Rupert.

'You need to report to the MovieDrome on Wednesday.'

'Seen the gate?' said Rupert brightly. 'Looks smart, doesn't it?'

Martin peered at the gate with astonishment, as though he'd entirely forgotten its existence.

'Oh, the painters came, did they?' he murmured at length. 'They didn't inform me.'

Rupert went round behind the gatehouse with the megaphone and sealed instructions to put them in our van. He didn't return for several minutes, during which time I endeavoured to hold a meaningful conversation with Martin. I noticed his suntan had faded completely. In fact, he was quite pale. He appeared distracted and showed scant interest in the newly-painted gate; or in the news that nobody had been to straighten up Baroness Turnpike. All he did was gaze vaguely in the direction of the Senior High School for Girls and nod his head. I was relieved when Rupert finally came back.

'By the way,' he said, 'will you be joining us at the MovieDrome on Wednesday?'

'Yes,' said Martin. 'I've been selected to represent the park authority.'

We asked if he'd like to stay for lunch but

he politely declined and was soon heading towards the coast.

'I wonder if they sunbathe at the independent settlement,' said Rupert.

'They probably don't have to,' I replied. 'From what I remember they were proposing an altogether different way of life. I imagine they work out of doors and acquire suntans naturally.'

'Sounds attractive, doesn't it?'

Rupert went into the gatehouse and came back with the map of the midland counties.

'There's been an idea at the back of my mind for a day or two,' he said, 'and now it's come to fruition.'

'Oh yes?'

'It strikes me as a bit selfish keeping this map to ourselves when other people might have need of it.'

'You mean people searching for the independent settlement?'

'Correct,' said Rupert. 'I think we should

put it on display somewhere, perhaps on the door.'

He unfolded the map and spread it out on the ground. We spent a few minutes studying the area shaded in pastel colours, and I had to admit it all looked very appealing. Rupert went inside and rooted through the cupboards in search of some drawing pins. It took a while, but eventually he found a few and we got the map pinned up.

We passed the afternoon idly watching semi-obsolete cars as they meandered among the potholes of the Great West Road. At dusk we went into the gatehouse, closed the shutters and stayed in all night. We didn't emerge until a couple of hours after daybreak next morning. When we opened the door we discovered that the map had been taken away. (The drawing pins had been considerately replaced in their holes).

'Not quite what I intended,' said Rupert, 'but never mind.'

Shortly after we'd finished breakfast, two black sedans drew up and parked opposite.

Carruthers stepped out of the first car; Presley and the other man remained inside the second.

Carruthers came over and we went out to meet him.

'I'm sorry to have to tell you,' he announced, 'that yours is a very mediocre little country. We've carried out an extensive survey during the past few months and our findings paint a sorry picture. The landscape is bland and uninspiring. The weather is unreliable. The beer is tepid. The roads are narrow. The rivers are sluggish. There are no proper mountains. No big skies. No untamed frontiers. No pioneers. No trailblazers. Nobody seeks adventure. Nobody runs any risks. In short, we've concluded that nothing exciting, interesting or unusual ever happens here.'

'Really?' said Rupert.

On the grass verge behind Carruthers were the recent tracks of at least four zoological species, all of them rather large, and all roaming free in the British Isles. For some reason, however, he'd failed to notice them.

'Anyhow,' he continued. 'Change of plan. We've been recalled to the homeland.'

'By the president?' I enquired.

'No, by his son-in-law.'

'Oh.'

'He's taken over all the day-to-day business.'

Carruthers peered at the shining gate.

'You're on your own now,' he said. 'There's nobody to help you.'

'That's alright,' I replied. 'Britain can stand alone.'

'I wouldn't be so sure,' he countered. 'You even have to import the ingredients for your cakes.'

He delved into a pocket.

'Catch,' he said, tossing Rupert the keys to his black sedan. 'You might as well have it now that it's surplus to requirements. We'll be leaving on the last flight out of here.'

Without a further word he joined his companions in the other car and they drove away. We watched them go.

'Kind of them,' I remarked.

'Yes, they're undoubtedly a generous nation,' said Rupert. 'It's just a shame they have to be so brash.'

We sauntered over to the black sedan and admired its finely upholstered interior. The vehicle was in perfect condition and it seemed a pity to let it go to waste.

'Tell you what,' I said. 'Why don't we take it for a drive?'

'We could do more than that,' said Rupert. 'We could go in search of the independent settlement.'

'Without a map?'

'Should be okay,' he said. 'I've more or less committed it to memory.'

A dazzling thought occurred to me.

'If we get there first,' I said, 'we can witness her grand arrival.'

We gathered up our few possessions and put them in the back of the car. Rupert slid behind the wheel and started the engine. I paused and glanced around before getting in.

'The road's very quiet today.'

'Yes.'

'What about the gate?'

'We'll leave it open.'

The author would like to thank Simon Moody for his patience.

Printed in Great Britain
by Amazon